FLOWER OF SPAIN

Jean Morrant

CHIVERS

British Library Cataloguing in Publication Data available

This Large Print edition published by BBC Audiobooks Ltd, Bath, 2009.
Published by arrangement with the Author.

U.K. Hardcover ISBN 978 1 408 45646 0
U.K. Softcover ISBN 978 1 408 45647 7

Printed and bound in Great Britain by
CPI Antony Rowe, Chippenham and Eastbourne

CHAPTER ONE

'Spain!' Vicky Hurst exclaimed, staring wide-eyed with amazement at the agency manageress.

'Is that too far?' Miss Garbutt asked, her brows raised. 'You did say you wouldn't mind going further afield in your next post. You haven't any ties,' Miss Garbutt went on. 'No one to object?'

'No,' Vicky stammered, 'but Spain! I hadn't thought of anywhere like that. Who wants a nurse in Spain?'

'A doctor, for his mother. Must have an English nurse.' Miss Garbutt explained, opening the buff file on her desk. 'We have all the references and details, so take a look, make up your mind. Good salary and conditions,' she added, in her usual business-like fashion.

Vicky studied the manageress for a moment. Miss Garbutt, trim, smartly dressed, efficient; one who wasn't to be let down on either side, references counted highly in her estimation. And Miss Garbutt was now becoming impatient.

'Yes, please,' Vicky blurted out. 'I'd like to know more about it,' and taking the neatly typed details, she studied them carefully.

On the Costa Dorada, she read, a villa on

the outskirts of the small town of Sitges. Temporary nurse/companion, three months (may be extended) required for elderly arthritic lady. Son, who is doctor with practice in Barcelona will be away for an indefinite length of time. Large modernised villa, household staff employed—own room with bath. Use of car. Senora Varela speaks English fluently. Urgent request for nurse to commence immediately. Doctor's private secretary, Senor Alvi, will receive and install suitably appointed person in her post on arrival in Barcelona.

The salary, Vicky noted, was much higher than usual.

'What did the last nurse leave for?' she asked.

'Instant dismissal I gather,' Miss Garbutt informed her. 'What do you think then?' she added briskly.

Vicky's mind worked quickly. 'How soon would I have to go?'

'Could you be ready by Saturday?'

'Yes, I'm sure I could.' Vicky spoke quickly, realising her previous, rather hesitant manner might appear that she lacked confidence.

She let her breath out slowly, hardly believing she'd made the decision and a slight feeling of apprehension rose within her.

* * *

A bitterly cold April wind blew across from the Pennines as Vicky entered Manchester Airport. Vicky had planned her wardrobe carefully. She had drawn rather heavily from the bank, planning to purchase new clothes on arrival. There was no need to scrimp and save now. No need to keep every penny for the trousseau she wouldn't need. She blinked back a tear; silly to think of Colin now. She mustn't let him into her thoughts any more, it wouldn't have worked anyway, yet she knew that marriage and Colin had been all she'd wanted not so very long ago until she'd gradually realised his feelings for her were beginning to wane.

He hadn't wanted to hurt her, he'd said, hadn't wanted to tell her, so she'd helped him out of his quandary and remembered the look of relief on his face. Relief he couldn't hide when she'd suggested they part for a while. He hadn't even 'phoned after that and she had known it was all over. Apart from needing employment, it was another good reason to leave England. Getting away from Colin, the memories, not seeing the familiar places they had visited together or, worst of all, having to face him in the village. Yes, it had been the right decision. The next three months would bring excitement, new happenings to replace old memories.

Once aboard the plane, Vicky relaxed, enjoying the new experience, watching buildings below decreasing in size and the river becoming a shining groove in the earth until they cut into low cloud.

'This is your first flight?' the well dressed man beside her asked, pleasantly.

Vicky nodded. 'Yes,' she said briefly, not wanting to take her eyes from the small window and become involved in conversation.

'Thought so. You appear too interested in what's going on for a seasoned traveller,' he remarked, flicking open a silver cigarette case.

She couldn't ignore him completely and gradually found herself drifting into conversation, learning his name was Mark Gildner and he was travelling to Barcelona on business. Vicky exclaimed in delight as they crossed the snow-capped Pyrenees and the sun reached down through breaks of cloud to reveal winding roads and tiny red roofed villages.

Mark smiled. 'Great country Spain. As you're new here, perhaps we could meet again?'

So quickly did the time pass with her new companion, Vicky was amazed when the signal was given to unfasten the seat belts. Trepidation rose within her. Soon the life she had anticipated for the past forty-eight hours would be reality.

As Vicky walked down the gangway steps, the calm, warm air met her, lifting her spirits higher. It was going to be all right. Any doubts were dispelled; there was no turning back now, only a growing excitement within her.

With her passport checked and luggage claimed, she walked through the neon-lit, marble floored airport hall in search of a taxi, plucking up courage to hopefully ask the grey uniformed policeman, 'Taxi.'

He nodded smilingly and, sticking his fingers between his teeth, let out a shrill piercing whistle in the direction of a car park opposite. Immediately a vehicle lurched forward, pulling up sharply beside her. The drivcr, a short stocky figure, jumped out and, taking her cases, quickly stowed them away in the boot.

The car set off at speed, manoeuvering between lanes of incoming traffic quite recklessly as, with her heart in her mouth, she fumbled in her bag for the address of her destination. As the driver read the address on the card, she found herself sitting forward in her seat, mentally willing him to slow down a little.

Gradually as she relaxed, Vicky looked out with interest as they entered Barcelona, travelling along mile upon mile of tree-lined road before they reached the busy city centre. She saw small parks and high playing fountains between lanes of swirling traffic; high buildings with splashes of colour lent by flowers cascading over the balconies. Traffic lights flashed and pedestrians swarmed, one halting, the other moving, alternately. The sun shone warmly through the car window, yet shaded areas between taller buildings brought a sudden chill to her. It was in such a narrow, shady street the taxi finally pulled up.

Smoothing down her skirt and fastening the jacket of her blue suit around her slim waist, she glanced at the name plates on the wall of the building. Doctor Varela's consulting rooms were on the first floor. She made her way up the wide marble staircase. Climbing the last few steps she paused, confronted by two dark wooden doors, each heavy with carving. Doctor Varela's name faced her from one door and taking a deep breath, she tapped. Her knuckles barely made a sound on the thick wood. She knocked louder, waiting for the summons to enter.

The large knob turned easily in her hand and the heavy door swung silently open across the gleaming tiled floor of a small waiting room. Ahead, another door, already open, revealed a high spacious room with shafts of sunlight shining in from the partly shuttered windows, on to a large polished desk which stood opposite. The few papers it held were laid in a neat pile. The black, heavily upholstered swivel chair behind was empty, as were the two high backed ones that faced it. Perplexed, she waited.

Suddenly, a tapping of typewriter keys came from behind a closed door on her left. So the place wasn't completely deserted after all! She went across to knock again.

'Sí?' a deep masculine voice demanded loudly and impatiently from within.

She opened the door to reveal a room lined with filing cabinets and, at the far end, a dark-haired man at a desk, pen in hand, poring over papers beside the typewriter.

'Sí?' the man demanded again without bothering to look up.

'Oh, do you speak English?' She stammered, taken aback by the harsh greeting.

Thc owner of the stern voice and dark hair looked up from his work, his brown eyes meeting hers momentarily before returning to the papers before him. Impatience mounted as she awaited his reply.

'Yes, a little,' he volunteered at last as he put down his pen. 'What do you want?'

'You must be Senor Alvi. I'm Victoria Hurst, I believe you are expecting me?'

His eyebrows lifted. He stood up, briefly gripping the hand Vicky offered. 'Yes. Please sit down, Miss Hurst.' He beckoned her to a chair, his eyes returning to his work.

'As the doctor is away, I bclicvc you arc the gentleman who will be taking me to Senora Varela's house,' she ventured and saw the corner of his mouth twitch with what she presumed to be amusement.

Was he laughing at her? To Vicky, this Senor Alvi appeared to be an ill-tempered, arrogant sort of fellow. Why didn't he answer more promptly, or didn't he understand?

'I am sorry I don't speak your language,' she said nervously. 'Did you understand?'

'You came early,' he replied coolly. 'I expected to be ready but these papers,' he pointed to the desk, 'they must be attended to. Also, you are much younger than the person I was given to expect. At first I thought you were a tourist needing a doctor's services.'

'Oh no, and I'm sorry if I am early,' she began apologetically, 'the plane arrived before time. I got a taxi immediately . . . '

'I shall not keep you very long, Miss Hurst,' he interrupted coldly, 'there are new plans I must explain to you.'

She watched him put the papers into a briefcase, with a growing impression that he resented her presence. Who did he think he was? She felt quite superior to this casually dressed Senor Aiyi, who didn't fit the picture of a super-efficient secretary at all. His shirt neck lay open, the sleeves were pushed carelessly up his arms, and she noticed, he even wore a pair of canvas shoes.

Determined not to be disconcerted by his cool attitude she casually remarked, 'I'm looking forward to my new post, although I wish I had been able to meet the doctor first.'

'Why?' he demanded sharply, glancing up, his eyes piercingly dark.

'Well, just to know what my duties would be.

What he expects of me.'

'I assure you, Miss Hurst, I am quite capable of giving you all the information on Senora Varela's affairs that you need to know.'

'Oh, I'm quite sure you are,' she retorted, feeling the colour rise to her cheeks, wondering why he should speak to her this way.

'Now,' he said, 'I will discuss the new plans with you. I can finish my work tomorrow.'

'New plans?' she queried, 'and tomorrow? Surely the doctor doesn't have you working on Sundays?' she added, hoping a little sympathy might help soften his manner.

'Like you, Miss Hurst, I must do as my employer wishes,' he declared, and Vicky felt sure she saw a gleam of amusement in his eyes.

He disappeared into what Vicky presumed to be the examination room. She sighed. Was this post going to result in being all she'd hoped for? This man had cast a shadow over her initial eagerness, bringing threads of doubt to her mind.

Vicky's thoughts were interrupted as he emerged, now looking well groomed, wearing a tie and light jacket. Even the canvas shoes had been replaced by shining leather. She watched him as he collected more papers from the filing cabinets, taking in the darkness of his freshly combed hair and the smooth tan of his skin. Apart from everything else, he was certainly a tall, good-looking man. Broad shouldered and clean shaven, he now had the appearance of being a very active and efficient man who, she guessed, would be in his mid-thirties.

Suddenly, she was aware of him watching her, with one dark eyebrow raised, he held her gaze for a second, before she glimpsed a scar beneath his chin.

'If you will pay attention, Miss Hurst, I will tell you about the change of arrangements,' he began, coming round the desk to sit on the edge of it. 'Senora Varela is at present residing in a hotel in Sitges, but this should not make much difference to your duties. I will explain.' He paused and held up his hand to silence the question she was about to ask, causing her to feel very small and defenceless as he looked down on her, dominating the silence.

'The chef and his wife who were employed at the Villa Barca were dismissed a while ago and have not yet been replaced, which left only one member of staff for the house. The gardener is there, of course, but that does not help with the problems of the kitchen, and until suitable replacements have been found, Senora Varela will stay in the hotel which she is familiar with, and I am sure you will also find it comfortable.'

'I'm sure I shall,' Vicky murmured, when he paused again.

He continued as if she hadn't spoken. 'There will be an adjoining room in the suite for your own use and, of course, you will take your meals there. I shall also arrange to escort you to the villa very soon so that you can familiarise yourself with the place.'

Vicky couldn't help but feel amazement that this man, who initially professed to speak only a little English, could reel off instructions in such detail. He interrupted her thoughts, his eyes questioning and cold.

'Nothing worries you, I hope?'

'Oh no, nothing, thank you,' she assured him, though discomfitted by his penetrating stare.

'Good. There is a small car at the hotel, for your own use. Your salary will be paid into the bank in the town square near to the hotel. I intend to bring it to your notice on the journey. Should you need to know anything more, you can always telephone me here.' He took a card from his pocket.

She thanked him. Though amazed by the efficient way he had dealt with everything, somehow he frightened her a little. She couldn't understand why she felt eager to please him but never seemed to succeed, and, most certainly, she wasn't accustomed to being spoken to in this curt manner by any man. He must not be allowed to intimidate her.

He carefully locked the doors and she meekly followed him down into the hall where he suggested she should wait, whilst he brought the car.

CHAPTER TWO

In minutes, a sleek black car purred by the doorway.

As he took her cases, Vicky asked, 'Do you mind? They are rather heavy.'

He glanced at her. 'There is no one else here to do it, is there?' came his sarcastic rejoinder, as he effortlessly swung the heavy baggage into the boot, and once more she felt the colour rise to her cheeks.

Sarcastic creature! Thank goodness she wouldn't be likely to see too much of him once she'd settled into the hotel. Murmuring her thanks as he closed the car door, she sat firmly upright in her seat, determined not to be provoked into saying anything she may later regret.

The car pulled away smoothly through the traffic-filled streets, southwards, leaving Barcelona behind.

Senor Alvi appeared to relax then, and slid sunglasses out of their case. She sensed his glance before he put them on, and now looking at him, his face seemed expressionless.

They travelled in silence for a while, yet there were moments when she sensed his eyes upon her, and it was when she caught his glance that he actually smiled, but then his eyes retained their steely gaze.

'You do not appear to have a great amount of luggage,' he commented, 'for three months.'

'Oh, I hope to buy one or two new dresses while I'm here. It will be nice to have something from Spain,' she told him, a surge of relief flooding through her. He was actually speaking in a much more pleasant tone.

'You think you will like it here, Miss Hurst?'

'Yes, I'm sure I shall. In any case, I will have to like it. It's not good for a nurse's reputation to take a post then let the patient down before the time is up, is it?'

He nodded in agreement, lifting Vicky's spirits.

'No, and I am very pleased to hear you have high principles,' he remarked, in a less stern voice.

So at last she had pleased him, for though she had been so determined not to let it bother her, she felt an easing of the tension within.

'Look, Senor Alvi,' she began, 'we probably won't see much of each other but—'

'No, I do not expect we shall,' he interrupted. Coolness edged his words again. Did he know what she had been about to say?

'And, by the way,' she retorted, 'there's absolutely no need for you to behave like some superior being in my company. I am only sorry you have the inconvenience of taking me to Sitges.'

There, she'd said it. Perhaps now he wouldn't keep up this stupid arrogant, bad-tempered air that he'd held from the first moment they'd met. She willed herself to relax, and looked out of the side window ready to ignore any further sarcasm her comments may induce.

'I will endeavour not to behave so,' came his quiet reply, which made her turn to look at him again. Now she couldn't fail to see a hint of amusement about this firm mouth, maddening her still further.

They passed through villages with narrow dusty roads, old houses which appeared to have balconies filled with washing, like bright flags drying in the sun, together with pots of colourful flowers hanging on the railings. Then the sea came into view; its blue like a deep reflection of the cloudless sky above. Vicky gasped with delight.

'Oh, it's beautiful!' she exclaimed, and suddenly realised she had broken the silence between them.

'I am glad it pleases you,' he commented.

Senor Alvi was silent again as they entered the little town of Sitges, driving the car capably as the traffic thickened in the narrow streets. He soon brought the car to a standstill outside a large and high building.

'We are at the hotel now. Please remain here one moment and I will get your cases.'

Vicky let out a sigh of relief. She was here at last. The thud of the closing boot made her turn, and he came to the window, pointing ahead, saying, 'Along there, and round the corner is the square where the bank stands. Be there at two o'clock tomorrow and I shall take you to Villa Barca, but do not say anything about this to the Senora. Understand?'

'But, why—' Vicky began.

'Please,' he silenced her, 'do not question everything. You will be free for two hours, and she will only be upset and want to go to her home. It is better she rests here. Also, she pefers no-one to learn of her whereabouts.'

'Are you not coming in Senor Alvi?'

'No, I have many things to do.'

'Who is going to introduce me to Senora Varela?'

'She is expecting you,' he said, impatiently. 'Until tomorrow, do not forget.'

Puzzled, Vicky got out.

He came and pressed the bell by the hotel doorway, saying only, 'Good afternoon, Miss Hurst,' before returning to the car and moving off at high speed.

* * *

Vicky looked up at the light stone building, the blue painted balconies laden with flowers. Above the door a decorative sign bore the name, 'Hotel Romantic.' In the doorway, a dark-haired young man was standing by her cases. He greeted her cheerily, and beckoned her to follow him inside, across the dimly lit hallway.

At the reception desk he paused. Behind it, stood a tall bearded gentleman.

The man smiled and introduced himself as the proprietor and, after examining her passport, escorted her to the first floor suite. Unlocking the door and swinging it open with a flourish, he stepped back for her to enter.

The room had a cool, quiet atmosphere, its walls white and clean. Sunlight pierced the slits in the shutters of the balcony window, revealing a brightly covered bed and coloured mats scattered over the shining tiled floor. She smiled and glanced towards the door opposite.

'That is Senora Valera's suite, through those adjoining doors,' he informed her. 'Would you like to meet the lady now?'

Vicky nodded, eager to meet the patient she had come so far to nurse, and he crossed to the centre doors, tapping on them lightly.

'Sí,' she heard, followed by a torrent of words in a language of which she knew so little. He paused in the doorway, giving a greeting in a similar tongue, and after hearing her own name announced, she stepped forward as the proprietor withdrew.

What Vicky expected her new patient to look like she had no idea, but on entering the adjoining room, she was pleasantly surprised. There, reclining in a huge leather upholstered chair was Senora Varela, beautifully elegant, a wide and welcoming smile on her face.

'Miss Victoria Hurst, I am delighted to welcome you,' she greeted, holding forth her hand.

It was immediately obvious the Senora was unable to move quickly and clung to her stick for support as she leaned forward. Vicky took the proffered hand. The touch of apprehensive shyness she experienced beforehand was quickly dispelled by the charming figure before her and she gave a warm greeting in return, adding an apology for her lack of knowledge of the lady's familiar tongue.

Senora Varela gently raised her hand. 'Please, I want to speak English to someone. I like to know about England, although it is many years since I visited. When I am interested no more, then I shall know I am old.'

Senora Varela told Vicky to sit in a nearby chair, then her dark beautiful eyes scrutinized the young nurse with interest before questioning her. She asked about the comfort of the journey which Vicky assured her had been wonderful, though she did not mention the cool reception of Senor Alvi.

'Go and look around the suite before lunch' she suggested. 'Then you will know this place we are to live in for a while.'

Vicky had already noticed this private lounge held comfortable furnishings, easy chairs, a carved Spanish table and chest of drawers which stood well against the pure whiteness of the walls, broken only by unusual colourful oil paintings, each heavily framed. The bedroom was like Vicky's own; another gay coverlet on the bed and beside it a similar table and lamp. An aroma of luxurious perfume reached her as she gazed at the assortment of well tailored clothes hanging inside the open wardrobe door.

She returned to the lounge and her smiling patient. The welcome she had received seemed more suited to a visitor. Everything around her was so different, the atmosphere warm; only faint sounds drifted up from the street below and the occasional shrill voice, interspersed with laughter, pierced the slits in the shutters outside the glass doors of the balcony.

'You must go and enjoy the sunshine in the afternoons if you wish,' the senora offered, 'but do be careful, you are so fair-skinned.'

Vicky nodded in agreement and they talked of the differing climates, the rain she had left behind; the older lady content to have fresh conversation. Eventually, her doctor son, who had left only days earlier, entered the conversation.

The dark eyes of Senora Varela held sadness as she spoke of him, a look of motherly concern spreading over her lovely face. A brighter expression returned as she talked of his work. He was such a busy man, so dedicated; the change of scenery at the convention in Gerona would do him a power of good. He would return refreshed.

Vicky asked about Senor Alvi but it appeared the senora had never met him, although she understood he was a very trustworthy man who, originally, had worked with her son's partner before they joined in practice.

Curiously intrigued, Vicky wanted to know more about Senor Alvi; ill-tempered though he was, he fascinated her in a strange way. She dismissed the thought as being purely one of curiosity. Even Senora Varela had agreed it was strange that he hadn't brought her up personally to introduce her, especially as he had finalised the arrangements and brought her to Sitges. She waved the idea aside, the diamond drops in her ears sparkling with her every movement as the narrow shafts of sunlight caught them.

'Gentlemen,' she said, 'even Spanish gentlemen, they are so strange. Paul also, he is like a boy sometimes.'

'Paul? Is he your son?' The Senora nodded, and Vicky concealed the amusement she felt. Somehow the little boy image didn't ring true of a professional man.

'Paul worries about me,' the senora continued, 'that is why he insisted on a qualified nurse rather than just a companion. I am not an ill woman, it is just these legs.' She looked down and grimaced. 'And my son is frightened I may fall if I am alone all the time, so I told him, if I must have someone, she must be intelligent and English. Someone I can have interesting conversations with,' she added, her smile returning.

'I hope I can come up to your requirements, Senora Varela. You must tell me about your treatment so that I can accustom myself to your routine.'

'I go to the clinic in Barcelona two or three times a week. You will accompany me and meet the Professor? He is a very clever man, already my walking is a little easier I am sure.'

'Yes, of course I will go. What kind of treatment is it?'

'He treats me with heat and warm water jets. It feels good, though I am very tired afterwards, Now, I want to know about you. You are younger than I expected.'

'I may be younger,' Vicky said laughingly, 'but I shall be very firm if I think it is best for you, and,' she added, 'I must know more about you. For instance, how well you can walk?'

'You shall see,' the older lady declared, reaching for her stick.

Leaning on it heavily, she heaved herself into a standing position and, even at full height, Vicky realised Senora Varela was only slightly taller than herself. Balancing reasonably well, once she had adjusted the position of her sticks, she took slow deliberate steps forward. Reaching the far wall, she turned slowly and began to tell Vicky of her daily routine.

'I shall need your help, Miss Hurst. It is harder for me to go down the stairs, but I am determined to do it—in fact,' she suggested, glancing at her watch, 'it is almost time to go now. I usually dine at one clock.'

Vicky went into her own room to freshen up, quite content with this initial meeting, any apprehension having been stemmed during the first few moments in Senora Varela's company.

It was a slow and tedious walk downstairs for the senora, but she complained very little. Vicky admired her spirit and gave verbal encouragement all the way to the cocktail bar where they rested on the cane chairs, sipping drinks. She learned the senora dined in her room in the evening as she found it more difficult to move around in the busy late hours. 'But you must come down for dinner, Miss Hurst,' she said firmly.

Vicky protested, quite willing to keep her company, but Senora Varela wouldn't hear of it, waving the idea aside, saying she ought to meet other people, make new friends here. 'You are young, I demand you come down here and enjoy the garden.'

Out in the soft warm air they ate a leisurely meal, discussing the menu and dishes Senora Varela liked. To Vicky it seemed more like a holiday atmosphere than one of work.

The lunch was delicious. Four courses of

excellent Spanish fare, followed by coffee. Later, Senora Varela decided she would return to her room and rest, suggesting her nurse may wish to do likewise. But Vicky was too wide awake, too interestingly aware of her new surroundings to consider resting and, leaving her patient lying comfortably on the bed, after promising to rejoin her for tea at four, she went to unpack.

There in her room, dresses hung away neatly in the wardrobe, she stacked the empty cases on top. Somehow the luggage reminded her of Colin; it would have held her trousseau, had everything gone according to plan not so many weeks ago. Strangely, the bitterness was diminishing; the hurt had almost gone, swept away by the miles she'd covered, and by having three months of unknown life ahead of her. And Mark Gildner? Perhaps it had been wise to decline his invitation. She tossed the card bearing his 'phone number aside. Here she was safe, her emotions would become calm and free.

Vicky decided on a look around the outside of the hotel and ran lightly down the stairs. Walking round the block, she realised the hotel took up a large portion of it after discovering the entrance to the garden in the next street, where she sat on the long bench with a shaft of sunlight playing down on her from between the trees. The hotel was silent. The only sounds came from trains passing through the little station two short streets away.

Doctor Varela must be very concerned for the safety of his mother to demand a qualified nurse's attention. It would be interesting to meet the man who was to pay so generous a salary each month and provided such a luxurious life-style. Senor Alvi appeared to think it unusual that she desired to meet her employer. She recalled his immediate reaction. Did he feel she undermined his own authority? His dark brown eyes penetrated her thoughts.

He caused her to feel inadequate, stupidly youthful and, in all probability, she had hurt his pride by having shown a little spirit in his company. She would not allow his arrogance to suppress or humiliate her ever, and tomorrow would be her next opportunity to prove it. He had offered no good reason as to why he wouldn't be calling for her at the hotel. Could it be business he had in Sitges, or work for the doctor?

Vicky found it difficult to dismiss Senor Alvi from her thoughts and even over tea, during conversation with Senor Varela, her mind wandered back to him. She inwardly reprimanded herself for caring as to what he thought of her, and it was the senora's question of where she had spent the afternoon that caught her attention.

'Just round the block, then I sat in the garden,' Vicky told her.

'Good. I expect you are tired but if you have energy after dinner, walk down to the sea, it will only take you five minutes. Turn left at the end of this street, and you will come to the square. Go down San Pablo and you are there. It is beautiful, the church is most prominent, standing by the sea.' Senora Varela gestured to indicate the course she wished her to take. 'I shall watch my television, Miss Hurst, so please, feel free. I may have a visitor, an old friend of mine, Senora Forteza. She frequently calls in the evening, particularly on the days I visit to the clinic, to inquire after my health.'

'Thank you. I hope I can learn a little Spanish while I'm here.'

'Catalan,' Senor Varela corrected her. 'Here we speak Catalan. It is quite different to the language of Spain. Many people here speak English now because of the tourism, although even with so many visitors, Sitges retains its air of sophistication. It is not yet spoiled.'

Later in the evening, after tidying the senora's room, Vicky went down to dinner. Through the doorway she saw daylight was fading and there, in the garden, coloured lights shone from the trees. Vicky followed the head waiter and, once seated, looked at the menu. She chose a mouth-watering dish and wine which Senora Varela had recommended.

She was suddenly aware of a man advancing her way, and immediately recognised him with a smile of surprise. 'Mark, I didn't expect to see you here.'

'Vicky! What are you doing here?' He showed equal surprise.

'Actually, I'm living here. It was unexpected but my patient is unable to live at the villa for a while so we're here instead,' she explained.

'No wonder I didn't get a reply.' He laughed. 'It's lucky I came here.'

'You've tried to ring me already?'

'Didn't want you to get away from me, or would you have rung me anyway?' He gave her a quizzical smile.

'Oh yes,' she assured him, guiltily remembering how she'd tossed his card aside earlier. 'Are you dining here?'

'Have done. I'm with a party of friends, and I'm afraid I must dash. When can I see you again?'

'Well,' she hesitated, 'I'm not sure of my routine yet.'

'Please say yes,' he begged. 'You're going to feel awfully alone here, you know. Consider me as an old friend and let me take you out.'

'Can I telephone you when I know I'm free?'

'Don't forget then, or I shall come looking for you.'

'I'll do that Mark,' she promised, 'as soon as I know.'

He moved swiftly towards the hotel bar, turning to wave as he mounted the steps.

After finishing her meal, Vicky decided on a

walk down to the beach.

She made sure Senora Varela was quite content, then donned a light jacket, and followed the directions given to her, finding the square easily. There was the bank where she was to meet Senor Alvi the next day, and after gazing up at the impressive building, she went on down San Pablo's narrow cobbled street flanked by shops, restaurants, and bars; a street brightly lit and filled with people taking an after-dinner stroll. San Pablo offered an unmistakably cosmopolitan air and there, at the end, was the sea, dark and silent in its flow.

The wide promenade flanked by tall palms stretched far to the right but on the left it came to a sudden halt at the floodlit church, the walls a mellow peach in colour, its profile clear and beautiful against the darkened sky. Even though she was captivated by the scene, Vicky resisted the longing to explore further; it was time to return to her patient.

As she turned to go back to the hotel, a long black car slid quietly to a halt on the road beside her. Vicky started. Surely it was the car she had travelled in earlier? The window lowered and there, in the driving seat was Senor Alvi. Before she could conceal her surprise and greet him, he spoke.

'What are you doing down here?' he demanded, curtly.

She stared at him in amazement. 'I'm just having a look around. Why?'

‘Alone?’ Again, his voice was cold.

‘Why yes, of course.’ She felt indignation pricking. ‘In fact I’m on my way back, though it’s really no concern of yours!’

‘Get in,’ he ordered, reaching over to the passenger door.

Vicky did as he asked and, once inside the car, glared at his stern face, but again he spoke first.

‘Who is with Senora Varela?’

‘No-one. I have only been out for a short while, and it was the senora who suggested it,’ she replied defensively, but with rising anger, added, ‘though I don’t see why I should explain my movements to you.’

‘I will drive you,’ he said, the cool edge leaving his voice and she observed his taut jaw line relax before he continued. ‘It is not suitable for you to walk out unescorted, Miss Hurst, especially as you are unaccustomed to the area.’

The anger within her subsided as she realised the reason for his concern. ‘It’s most kind of you to be so concerned, Senor Alvi, but I will be careful, and also if the doctor ever asks you, I would never leave Senora Varela unaccompanied for any length of time.’

He nodded. They were near the hotel very soon and, alighting from the car, she thanked him, adding how beautiful a place she found Sitges to be. Her words seemed to please him. A slight smile touched his firm lips, the dark eyes softened a little in the glow of the interior light as he wished her goodnight.

The memory of those eyes stayed with her as she walked from the corner of the block to the hotel door.

CHAPTER THREE

Senora Varela hadn't used the night bell specially installed to call her nurse, so it was the bright morning light that awoke Vicky. As she pulled a brush through her hair before fastening it up into the usual soft roll, she considered her duties to her patient, hoping to broach the subject of her routine over breakfast.

'Good morning, Senora Varela,' she greeted politely, setting down the breakfast tray.

The senora smiled. 'As you are also my companion, need we be so formal? You are so young, I would like to use your forename. It is Victoria, is it not?'

'Yes it is, but I usually get Vicky.'

The senora smiled, saying how helpful it would be to have regular assistance with her morning shower, and such a pleasing companion to chat with over breakfast. She had relied on the help of her elderly friend, Senora Forteza, after the last companion left so suddenly. The reason for her departure remained a mystery to Vicky and Senora Varela seemed reluctant to discuss the details. She then went on to tell Vicky of her appointment at the clinic in Barcelona next morning.

Hearing Barcelona mentioned, reminded Vicky of Mark. There was time to telephone him before her meeting with Senor Alvi.

Delighted to hear her voice, Mark asked, 'Why don't we meet tonight, Vicky? I'll come and have dinner with you.'

A spark of excitement rose. At least Mark would be pleasant company, unlike the haughty and hostile Senor Alvi.

After lunch, Vicky tidied herself in preparation for her appointment with the dark Spaniard. It seemed strange he should wish to meet her by the bank and not come and pay his respects to the mother of his employer.

She set off in the direction taken the previous evening. Across the road, opposite the bank, stood the sleek, black car. She was two minutes late and, nearing the vehicle, Vicky saw his fingers drumming on the steering-wheel, a look of impatience on his face.

'Good afternoon,' she greeted him brightly, on reaching the open car window.

He looked up, silent for a moment, finally acknowledging the greeting as he got out to hold the door.

'How are you finding your new position

here?' he asked suddenly.

'Well, its hard to say really, I don't . . .'

'You do not like it?' he interrupted sharply.

'No, let me finish. I was going to say, I don't feel it is like work, it's more like a holiday. Senora Varela is charming but there seems so little to do for her; not that it counts exactly, as I want to encourage her to do most things for herself. I suppose it's more companionship I'm giving her. In fact, I wonder why the doctor required a qualified nurse.'

'You are bored, would you say?' he rejoined sharply.

'Oh no, it's exciting here. The hotel is first class, and I have a lovely room. I had a short drive in the car this morning, which reminds me, Senor Alvi, can you tell me how I can get in touch with my employer?'

'Is this request urgent?' His tone was brisk.

'No, not really. There are a number of things I'd like to ask the doctor concerning his mother's treatment and general welfare, but I think it would be better if she was not aware of my asking.'

'Why not,' he snapped, 'are you thinking of changing everything?'

'Certainly not!' she retorted, 'and please do not question my professional judgment. I only wish to ask him if he would consider outings in my car, and more meals taken in the dining room downstairs, plus a suitable diet, more agreeable to her condition. Believe me, Senor

Alvi, my thoughts are purely for the welfare of my patient,' she added, her cheeks growing hot with annoyance.

'I apologise, Miss Hurst,' he said quietly, taking Vicky by surprise. 'If you care to give me a letter, I will make sure you get a reply.'

Calmed a little by his apology, Vicky remembered her vow not to rise to his provocation. But maybe it was a good idea not to allow him to escape his rudeness without rebuke.

'Very well,' she replied calmly. 'I suppose you forward his mail so I'll send it to Barcelona. It's just that I don't want to do anything he doesn't approve of or, of course, anything which would upset Senora Varela. Doctors do vary you know, some are sticklers for medical routine, whereas others consider their patient's happiness a little more. In this case it is his mother so I'm not sure what he prefers. Really, I'm sorry I missed him. What sort of a man is he?'

Senor Alvi puckered his lips thoughtfully, and it was a few moments before he answered. 'It is difficult to say, Miss Hurst. I presume his patients have confidence in him; he has a large practice. I cannot really tell.'

This was the only information she gained. He appeared reluctant to add more. Vicky sighed. Senor Alvi was the most exasperating man—so unlike Mark Gildner—not the slightest bit pleasant or cheerful. Thank goodness, she could relax in Mark's company this evening and quieten the tension within her. At this moment her nerves were taut, and she was completely on edge.

They were turning out of the town when the buildings changed their outline. Instead of high terraces shading the streets, she saw low detached villas set in large gardens.

He pointed ahead saying, 'Many of these villas are not very old but you see the one on the hill, standing alone? That is the Villa Barca.'

Vicky shaded her eyes and saw the large villa, with a high wall surrounding its grounds. Trees sheltered it on the inland side, partly hiding the tall grey building and, as they wound up the dusty narrow road, nearing the house, she noticed its upper windows were completely shuttered.

Bringing the car to a halt beside the long wall he got out, and unlocking the heavy iron gates, swung them wide. Once inside, on a pebbled drive, he immediately went back to lock the gates, and it occurred to Vicky he seemed to be taking no chances of anyone trespassing on his employer's property.

Now Vicky could observe the lower windows were also heavily shuttered, even the smallest had iron grilles across them. But the balconies were hung with bright foliage; the only outward sign of life on this fortress-like building.

Senor Alvi inserted a large key into the lock of the deeply carved door. It swung open slowly, heavy on its hinges.

Standing inside the tiled hall, she shuddered, feeling the cool, still air envelop her in the silent semidarkness. 'Please open the shutters, Senor Alvi, I can't see very much.'

'You English and your sunlight,' he scoffed. 'The shutters must remain locked.' Instead, he switched on the light and the hallway suddenly became quite beautiful, as shadows thrown from the huge crystal chandelier patterned the ceiling and walls.

'Oh, it's beautiful,' she said, seeing his expression soften, as though he gained pleasure from her appreciation. But the momentary sign vanished when she continued, 'If I lived in Spain, I would want to throw open all the windows.'

He frowned slightly. 'Not in mid-summer, you would be glad of the coolness. The shutters are always closed by lunch time, especially in the south where early in the day the floors are washed with cold water to keep the heat at bay, not as in your country, you do not have such high temperatures.'

He had taken off his dark glasses, and since their first meeting in the doctor's office she had not seen the thick arched brows over his eyes. As though he sensed her studying him he glanced away quickly, suggesting they should see the rest of the villa.

The downstairs lounges were spacious and the furnishings there hidden from view under large white dust sheets. In the kitchen, royal blue patterned tiles contrasted with rows of shining pots and pans and, from the sink, polished brass pipes gleamed their way along to the outer wall. The cooker looked large and mysterious. Senor Alvi explained it was typically Spanish, but central heating had been installed to give extra comfort during the winter now Senora Varela was not quite so mobile.

'You seem to know more about Senora Varela than she does of you,' Vicky commented.

He glanced down at her sharply but didn't reply.

'Do you know when I'm likely to be moving in here?' she asked, as they ascended the wide staircase.

'You will be informed,' he told her archly.

Gripping the ornamental handrail to stifle her indignation, she followed him on to the landing where he pointed to each closed door in turn—the guest suite, the senora's rooms and there, he pointed to the end door, was her own room.

'And the doctor's?' she questioned.

In reply he nodded towards the other end of the landing.

'Can I see my own room?' she asked eagerly.

'Certainly.' He gestured for her to go in, his eyes following her.

It was another large room, comfortably furnished, and not unlike the one at the hotel. She inspected it, slowly wandering around: yes, she could settle in here easily.

She found Senor Alvi standing by a small unshuttered window on the landing.

'It's lovely,' she told him. 'I hope it won't be too long before we move in. Really, it's a beautiful house.'

A faint smile moved his lips. 'You will like it, that is good.'

'Can't I tell the senora I've seen it yet?'

'No.' He sounded emphatic. 'Not until you are directed to do so.'

'There is no need to speak to me that way,' she retorted crossly, her cheeks growing warm.

'Senora Varela frets for her home, I understand, Miss Hurst. We do not want to upset her, do we? Come,' he added, beckoning her to the window.

Vicky found the view to be breathtaking; sleepy white houses below, palm trees lining the narrow road, the blue sea beyond.

'Oh, it's all so beautiful,' she said, and, turning towards him with a smile, found he wasn't sharing the view. He was staring at her intently.

He quickly diverted his stare but not before she glimpsed the expression in his dark eyes. They had seemed to hold sadness, maybe even pain. What was he thinking? Even though he'd hurt her frequently by his curt manner during their short time together, a strange sympathy rose within her, causing a desire to break his cold outer shell and discover what lay beneath.

'Where do you live?' she asked, making a greater effort to be friendly towards him. 'Do you have a family in Barcelona

'No, I live alone there, Miss Hurst,'

'Please call me Vicky. The senora does and, after all, I suppose we are colleagues, in a way. What is your name?' She smiled up at him, wisps of fair hair falling against the milky skin of her slim neck.

A brief smile touched his lips. 'As you wish. You may call me Ramon.'

She wished to keep the conversation going in this lighter vein, wanting to see him smile again but suddenly, it was hard to find the right words. With a nervous laugh, she rushed on, 'I'm quite looking forward to meeting this mystery employer of mine, though I feel he may be a rather fearsome character. What do you think, Ramon?'

'I am sorry, Miss Hurst, I do not wish to discuss your employer,' he replied, a grave face returning as he ushered her towards the stairs.

'Naturally, I'm only interested in the man because he employs me,' she replied tartly, 'and please stop calling me Miss Hurst,' she added. 'You make me feel quite an old spinster.'

'Perhaps it would be better if you were so,' was his cool reply.

She couldn't understand Ramon, he could be reasonably pleasant, then for so little reason, would become cool and distant. It was infuriating, but she must be as tolerant as possible. The doctor would not receive a bad report. She frowned as it occurred to her that perhaps the doctor had asked Ramon to keep an eye on his mother's nurse. If so, she would make sure there wasn't anything he could find fault with as far as her care of Senora Varela was concerned.

Ramon glanced at his watch. 'Come, Vicky,' he urged, 'there is also the garden to see.'

Outside again, returning by way of thc hall, with the big door securely locked behind them, they walked across well kept lawns to the rear of the villa. Ramon was silent, no light conversation, no laughter, as though he didn't welcome her company. This visit was just a duty he had to perform. His expression revealed little, being partly hidden behind the dark spectacles again, but he had called her by her first name once, however reluctant he'd been to use it.

At the rear of the house, a large pool lay calm and inviting, sheltered by the high outer walls and the gentle acacia trees. This area was a sun trap, an ideal place for her spare moments and she longed to plunge her slim body into the refreshing clear water.

On the return journey, Ramon pointed out places of interest, and she felt it a pity he wasn't more approachable. She could learn so much more about local history from someone who knew it so well, or was he the one least likely to enlighten her? There was nothing to be lost by asking him.

'When you come this way again, I would like to join you during my free time.' She smiled hopefully. 'It would give me an opportunity to get to know the district.'

He turned towards her silent for a moment, his lips firm and unsmiling. 'I hope you will not approach anyone else this way, Miss Hurst, just to satisfy your thirst for knowledge of the area.'

'Certainly not,' she retorted. 'Are you also acting as my protector?'

'No, but I would not wish you to harm your reputation by your naivety.'

'Really, I have . . .' she began, but he raised a finger to silence her.

'I also think only of the senora, Miss Hurst.'

*   *   *

Mark was already waiting when she reached the lounge that evening. Smiling broadly, he stood to greet her, impeccable in a smooth, well tailored suit. Taking her hand he led her down the steps to the colourfully lit garden.

'I've looked forward to meeting you again

all day,' he declared, holding her chair. 'Perhaps we can go on to a show later?'

'Oh, I really don't think so. My patient is alone. Her friend will not be calling this evening, but thank you all the same.'

'Another night maybe?' he proposed, before giving their order.

'Yes, I'll try and arrange it,' she agreed, a little cautiously. 'Are you here for very long?'

'Here most of the time, actually. I do go to London occasionally.'

'What kind of business are you in, Mark?'

'I'm with an agency,' he told her. 'You could say, advertising.'

She was glad of Mark's company and happily related her simple life story. Time passed quickly, and by nine-thirty, Vicky decided it was time to return to Senora Varela.

She strolled with him to where his car was parked, by the garden entrance. He dropped a light kiss on her cheek. 'I'll be here again tomorrow evening,' he promised. 'Arrange to stay out a little later, if you can.'

Somewhat bewildered by Mark's eagerness, she smiled as he drove off down the narrow street. He was certainly good company, possessing an easy going charm which proved very relaxing. She was glad he would be coming again tomorrow, but felt it wiser not to mention it to Senora Varela so soon.

CHAPTER FOUR

The next morning, Vicky helped Senora Varela prepare for her visit to the clinic. The route they took to Barcelona was quite different, compared with the one hugging the coast which Ramon had used when he brought her to Sitges. This road was wider; factories lay, large and busy on the flat land, all so different from the stretches of lazy sand and shimmering blue water of the coastal route.

The clinic looked impressive as they drove through the gates, so fresh and white, set in green lawns. Senora Varela introduced her doctor, Professor Forteza, husband of the lady who came to sit and chat with her occasionally, then, returning her attention to Vicky, said, 'I want you to go into the city and collect the jewellery I had repaired. Will you?'

Vicky nodded. 'Of course.'

'Good. You will not get lost. Alfons will wait for you. I shall not be ready until midday, so enjoy your free time.'

Alfons drove into the town at a much faster pace, skilfully weaving and winding between the heavy traffic, along the Paseo de Gracia and, turning left, he parked the car. Gesticulating towards the main street he indicated the jewellers Senora Varela wished her to call on. 'I wait here,' he said jerkily, and pointed, first to the car, then to his watch.

It gave Vicky almost two hours to look round after she had done her errand. The shops were grand and plentiful, enough to while away the time.

Wandering along the wide pavement she gazed at the goods on display, and it was only when she was about to cross at a junction, on pausing for the green light, she suddenly realised the street on her right was where the doctor's practice stood. A curious surge of excitement rose. Ramon may be there; should she call? Inspiration came quickly. She hadn't written the letter for him to forward to Doctor Varela, there had not been time this morning, but now it would give her good enough reason for calling.

Presuming he would be in his office again, and wouldn't hear her knock on the outer door, Vicky walked straight into the waiting room. She stopped quickly as, through the partly open consulting room door, she saw Ramon sitting there, his elbows on the large desk, his head resting on his hands. Her immediate reaction was one of concern. Was he unwell, or only deep in thought? She tapped lightly.

He glanced up quickly, and for a moment his expression was tense until he recognised his visitor, when his features relaxed.

Making an effort to gather his composure, he rose and came round to close the door behind her. 'Is something wrong, Vicky? Is there anything you need?'

She explained her reason for visiting, and the errand for Senora Varela. He looked relieved and supplied her with writing paper on which Vicky listed, in her most professional manner, ideas she had concerning the senora's welfare. She wished to gain the doctor's approval on these.

He offered coffee, suggesting they take it in his office, thus allowing him to continue with his work, he explained. She accepted gladly, and very soon, heard a tray being delivered to the consulting room.

Ramon, bringing in the tray, set it before her. 'Will you pour?'

'Where did you learn such good English?' she asked, reaching for the handle of the silver jug.

'University,' he said briefly, turning quickly as he heard her quick intake of breath, her gasp of pain as she let the jug drop back on to the tray with a clatter. 'What is it? You are burned?'

'Yes I am.'

'Come,' he ordered, taking hold of her wrist, leading her into the next room where he quickly thrust her reddened palm under the cold tap.

As the cool water soothed the pain in her hand she became aware of his grip. The smoothly tanned fingers curled firmly around her slim pale wrist. She glanced up, catching sight of the long red scar once more. Patting away the excess moisture with a cotton swab, he opened her hand gently. 'Does it hurt so much now?'

Vicky found his soothing tone disturbing as he examined her palm. 'It's much better, thank you,' she said shakily. 'It was silly of me not to think of it being so hot.'

'No, no, I should have thought, Vicky,' he apologised, his hand lingering on hers as their eyes met, 'but I do not think it will blister.'

Amazed that this tall, usually brusque mannered man should suddenly show such a gentle and sympathetic side to his nature, she allowed him to escort her to a chair. His unexpected tenderness caused her almost to forget her gratitude and assure him she was quite all right.

Suddenly she wanted to learn more of this city, longed to see what it offered the visitor. Mark had offered, almost insisted he should act as her guide but, curiously, it was Ramon's company she preferred. The warmth she experienced, brought about by his kindness, made her feel less of a stranger. She was part of this life now.

Turning, she caught him staring at her, his eyes searching. He glanced away quickly as she spoke. 'Ramon, do you have much spare time?'

'Very little, why?' he asked, guardedly.

'Please don't think it forward of me but I would like to see more of Barcelona whenever I have the opportunity, though it's so large, I'm sure I would get lost. Even if you haven't time, perhaps you could suggest the best places to see.'

He appeared quite taken aback by her request, and she heard his quick intake of breath. It was seconds before he answered. 'I doubt if this will be possible, Vicky. I have much work to do.' He paused a moment, as though considering it a problem.

'If you are really interested,' he added, 'and determined, then it is better if you do not go alone. Barcelona is a beautiful city with much to offer. I will try,' he promised, and, after another examination of her hand, plus a further assurance from Vicky that she was quite all right, he ushered her to the door.

Strolling back towards the waiting taxi, a smile touched her lips. She was pleased he had been less formal towards her this morning, but wondered why he presented such a distraught picture when she had first entered.

Senora Varela was not quite ready when Vicky reached the clinic so she acquainted herself with the reception area, struggling to understand the explanatory notices, and listening to the quick chatter of the nurses in crisply starched uniforms as they advanced towards incoming patients or escorted outgoing ones to the wide front hall.

'Here is your little English nurse,' Vicky heard, and turned to see Professor Forteza with Senora Varela. He wished them a safe journey and, to the senora, special good wishes to her son, hoping he was fully recovered.

Vicky hesitated in her step. What did he mean? Had Doctor Varela been ill, or had an accident? It was strange the senora hadn't mentioned it.

Curiosity made her question Professor Forteza's words as they returned.

'It is nothing,' Senora Varela murmured, lapsing into thoughtful silence for the remainder of the journey.

After lunch, Vicky tried the car again, and drove carefully down towards the beach. Having been so fascinated by this scene the first evening, she wanted to see how it compared in the daytime.

Sitting on the steps which led down to the beach, she looked up at the church behind. Today it stood tall against a cloudless sky. Basking in the warm sun, she allowed her thoughts to drift back to the morning and Ramon. The moment of kindness, the concern over her hand being burned and, looking down at her slightly reddened palm, she smiled. Did it take something in the nature of an accident, however slight, for him to be pleasant towards her?

When Vicky returned for tea, she heard the murmur of Senora Varela's voice from the next room. Thinking Senora Forteza had visited early, she settled down to write a letter to Miss Garbutt to let her know she was quite happy here and put her mind at rest.

Suddenly, the voice next door rose, filled with distress, then silence. She listened for a moment. The faint tinkle of a telephone bell told Vicky it was not at her friend, Senora Varela aimed her emotional outburst.

Putting her pen and paper aside, she ventured into the adjoining room to find Senora Varela displaying an expression of utter despair.

'Are you all right, Senora?' Vicky asked gently, seeing tears well up in the lovely brown eyes. 'At first I thought Senora Forteza was with you.'

Senora Varela let her hands fall to her lap in a disconsolate gesture. She shook her elegant head slowly. 'It was my son on the telephone,' she blurted out. 'He makes me so sad, but I can do nothing.' Her hands expressed her resignation.

Puzzled as to what Doctor Varela could possibly have done to upset his mother so, Vicky waited for her to continue with growing curiosity.

'I am sorry, Vicky, I cannot tell you,' she continued. 'Senor Alvi, he has not spoken of Paul?'

Vicky shook her head.

'Obviously, he is a very loyal servant,'

Senora Varela declared with satisfaction. 'You will not speak of my distress?'

'No, certainly not,' Vicky assured her.

'Good. A Catalan has so much pride.'

Senora Varela leaned forward and looked intently into Vicky's eyes. 'That is why you are here, little English girl. Paul wanted someone here with me when he must go away to the conference. But I want to go back to my villa, and I told him so today. I want to return to my own home, and he must come back also.'

As Vicky dressed for dinner, the senora's obvious distress troubled her. Doctor Varela had become a character to dislike, even before meeting him. She couldn't be sure the post would remain as pleasant on his return, and it wasn't possible to question Ramon, not now, when she'd given a promise.

Again, Mark awaited her arrival in the lounge, wearing a different but equally well tailored suit. Throughout dinner, he asked about her day with interest, laughingly reprimanding her for not contacting him during her free time. Secretly, Vicky was glad she hadn't. Spending the time with Ramon had been so worthwhile, when his usual aloofness had been discarded to reveal sympathy and tenderness.

She declined Mark's offer of a late show after dinner. Instead they strolled down to the beach where the night air was still and heavy with the scent of flowers. He took her hand as they reached the paved promenade to walk towards the church, its illumination casting irregular shadows through the palms. By the steps, they paused to look out to sea, and he pulled her closer, the warmth of his hands penetrating her thin dress.

Glancing up at his regular features she met a ready smile. 'I'm so pleased we met, Vicky. Just think, if I'd taken any other plane this would never have been. Already, I'm very fond of you.'

'Mark, we've only just met,' she said, a little overwhelmed by his enthusiasm. 'You don't really know me, and I know so little of you.'

She tensed slightly for one moment, sure he was about to kiss her, but he just held her gaze and smiled. It was the first time she had met a man so suave and confident and she enjoyed his courteous attentions.

Quite suddenly, and unaccountably, Ramon entered her thoughts, his darkness blotting out Mark's fair, well groomed image, disturbing her so deeply she had to speak and break the reverie. 'Can we walk over there?' She pointed to the brightly lit row of shops and bars on the other side of the promenade.

'By all means, but I'd prefer it if you would allow me to take you into that bodega. We could take wine and listen to the music.'

The bodega bar, its interior lined with bottles and barrels of varying shapes and sizes, was filled with the aromatic smell of cigars.

When they were comfortably seated, her eyes rested on Mark to observe the heavy gold ring he wore, as he took a cigarette and flicked open his lighter. Glancing over the immaculate suit once more as he slid the lighter into his pocket, she judged him to be a very successful businessman. It was rather exciting to be in the company of such a sophisticated person, and his courtesy appeared beyond reproach.

'Can I meet you again, Vicky?' he asked later, as he escorted her back to the hotel. 'I'm a little tied up at weekends, but I do need to see you, so much. Say you will, please?'

'I'm not sure when I'm free, Mark.'

'Then I'll telephone you,' he promised, before getting into his low white sports car and driving away.

It was on Thursday morning, when she went down for the breakfast tray, a little earlier because of the pending visit to the clinic, that the proprietor met her with a letter, bearing a Barcelona post mark. This must be the doctor's reply, Vicky guessed.

Upstairs, in her own room, she slit open the envelope. It contained two separately folded sheets of paper, the first a brief note from Ramon, asking her to call when she next visited the clinic; the other, typewritten, professionally worded, agreeing with her suggestions concerning the senora. The signature below was unrecognisable, although Doctor P. Varela was typed beneath. She felt relieved the suggestions had met with his approval.

She looked again at the first note, the handwriting bold and clear, signed only 'Ramon,' and a surge of pleasure ran through her at the prospect of meeting him again.

CHAPTER FIVE

Dressing carefully to suit the warm, sunny weather Vicky chose a light cream blouse, pleated skirt and matching sandals. Ramon had been foremost in her mind since she read his note, but suddenly, it crossed her mind that he may be married or engaged.

At the clinic, slightly tense with anticipation, she bade Senora Varela farewell, promising to return by midday. Almost at the corner of the street, which led to the doctor's practice, she paused, to look in the window of a gown shop, feasting her eyes on a beautiful blue chiffon dress. Suddenly aware of someone standing close behind her, she glanced up to find Ramon reflected in the glass.

'Are you planning to spend your salary already?' he asked, pleasantly.

Turning in time to catch a smile playing on his lips, her pulses quickened, and she couldn't conceal her pleasure at seeing him here so unexpectedly. 'Hello,' she said brightly, 'are you having a morning off?'

Not entirely, there was a little business to attend to before you arrived. Shall we take coffee first?'

This time, when the tray arrived, he poured, reminding her of the last occasion.

'How is your hand now, Vicky?' he enquired.

'Oh, er, fine, thank you. Perfectly all right now,' she stammered, quite overcome by his charming manner.

Remembering her doubt concerning his status, she considered this a suitable time to bring the matter forth. 'Thank you for the doctor's letter, Ramon,' she began. 'I'm pleased he is agreeable. I had an awful thought when I got your note, though.' She paused, apprehensively. 'I asked you to show me round and,' she hesitated, 'maybe you're engaged, or even married? I don't want to cause you any embarrassment.'

He put his cup down quickly. She saw his face darken as he stood up and turned to stare out of the window. 'No,' he said, quite firmly, a muscle twitching on his jaw. 'You cause me no embarrassment, Vicky.'

Vicky was curious. Had she touched a nerve? Whatever he had felt for that moment however, was soon cast aside as he told her of the places they would visit, and that being the reason for his invitation, they had better hurry and make the most of the two hours she had free.

As they were about to leave his office there was a loud knock on the outer door. He hesitated. 'Wait here one moment please,' he said, quickly closing the door behind him.

Voices from the consulting room came clearly to the office where she waited. Clear, but unrecognisable—did she hear the word 'police'? She heard Ramon laugh, and his words of thanks, as though they were spoken in relief.

Soon he returned, smiling, and carrying a small, flat box which he put into the safe.

She wondered who his callers had been to bring such a look of elation to his face—there was definitely something different about Ramon this morning. But now, as he helped her down the steps to the underground trains, he was like any other carefree escort, pointing out places of interest, smiling, and giving her his every attention.

They left the metro at the Plaza de Cataluña, with its central paved island, broken here and there by fountains, trees and flower beds. 'Most of the metro and railway lines converge here,' he told her. 'Day and night the traffic swirls around the centre.'

'It seems such a busy city, Ramon, but exciting. It's also a little frightening,' she added, relieved that he took her arm as they went over the crossing.

He looked down and smiled, bringing to her

a surge of pleasure as his hand stayed at her elbow, helping her through the crowd.

The street narrowed, and soon the spires of the cathedral were in sight. As they drew closer, it towered above them. 'This building was begun at the end of the thirteenth century,' he informed her, as they looked upwards. 'We must come back one evening when the delicate spires are illuminated, and light from inside glows through the stained glass windows.'

'It's magnificent,' Vicky said, in admiration.

'I am sorry we have no time to go inside today,' he apologised, but continued to bring to her notice other points of interest as they strolled along.

He turned towards her. 'This area we call the Gothic Quarter, so named because many of the buildings were constructed between the thirteenth and fifteenth centuries, but it is much older.'

'You're quite a historian, Ramon,' she told him, as they paused again in one of the many majestic courtyards.

The cool air in the high, narrow alleyways caused him to look at her with concern. 'Are you cold? Come, we will soon be in the sun.'

Taking her hand, they walked along more quickly, turning into the warm air by the port, back towards the centre. He pointed ahead to the wide tree-lined avenue, 'Barcelona's best known promenade,' he informed her, and they strolled along the central walkway.

He observed her quietly, while she exclaimed in delight at the stalls of flowers, heavy with colourful blooms, and others filled with books and magazines. Never before had she seen such an avenue as this, in a continuous state of bustle, full of colour, light, and movement.

'Ramon,' she held his sleeve, 'will you wait a moment, please. I would like to take some flowers to Senora Varela.'

Quickly he laid his hand upon hers as she was about to open her bag. 'Please allow me,' he begged her, and purchased two bunches of carnations from the nearest stall.

She thanked him and gazed at the beautiful red blooms, breathing in their sweet scent. 'Oh, Ramon, how nice of you. Thank you, they're lovely.'

He gazed down on her and smiled. 'I hope you like them. We call them Clavel, the flower of Spain. Come, we must hurry,' he urged.

She glanced back down the long avenue. This was one of the loveliest places she'd seen. Almost breathless with delight, she thanked him warmly, enthusing over the pleasures of the morning.

'Maybe one day, you would like to go to Montjuich by car and see the city from the mountain?' he suggested.

'Oh yes, please, Ramon, I'd love to.'

As he took her hand to wish her goodbye,

she felt a fresh surge of pleasure. Was it in anticipation of the sight-seeing, or was it the prospect of another meeting with Ramon?

* * *

As Vicky went down for dinner that evening, there was a telephone call for her at the desk, and her heart leapt at the sound of Ramon's voice.

'Are you tired after your long walk this morning?' he asked.

A little,' she admitted, 'but I enjoyed it so much.'

'Then may I suggest something a little more restful? Will you have dinner with me tomorrow evening?'

A sudden glow of happiness surged through her whole being.

'Here do you mean, Ramon?'

'No,' he replied, quickly, 'not Sitges. I will meet you near the station, you know where it is?'

'Yes, thank you. Senora Varela has a friend coming tomorrow, so I'm sure it will be all right.'

'Good, and as you usually dine alone, it may make a pleasant change for you. There are many excellent hotels nearby.'

She thanked him for his invitation, feeling delighted at the prospect of sharing an evening with him, but his final words surprised her.

‘Perhaps it is better you do not mention it to Senora Varela,’ he suggested and, rather reluctantly she agreed, promising to be by the station at seven o’clock.

Mark was a little later than usual, and most apologetic for the delay. As usual, he was charming, and most attentive, but sorry he wouldn’t be able to join her the following evening, due to an appointment, he explained. Relieved she didn’t find it necessary to refuse meeting him the following evening, she agreed to his suggestion to telephone her on Monday.

He took both her hands. ‘You’re not upset because I can’t come to see you over the weekend, are you, darling?’

‘Of course not, Mark,’ she assured him, and noticed it was his turn to look relieved. Was he becoming so fond of her that it mattered to him if she should be upset?

* * *

At three minutes to seven the following evening, the long dark car was already standing by the station, and Vicky smiled as she drew nearer. Ramon regarded her admiringly, but made no comment as he held the door.

They drove in the direction of the hills beyond Sitges, finally pulling up beside a small hotel, which was partially concealed by a profusion of natural growth. It was an enchanting place, low lit and tastefully decorated.

'Do you like it here?' he asked when they were seated. 'I believe this hotel has a very good chef, but the menu is in Spanish. Shall I translate?'

'Please, Ramon, but suggest something for me, will you?'

'Then it is the traditional Catalan cuisine for you tonight,' he declared. 'Yes, I think you will like that.' He went on to explain what dishes he would order and their ingredients.

'It all sounds lovely,' she told him, trying to remain calm and willing her heart to stop its unaccountable fluttering. Why was it she found it easier to converse with him when he wasn't so pleasant and courteous?

He smiled briefly, and returned his attention to the menu. 'Will you have more wine?' he asked, but without waiting for her reply, bade the waiter pour it into their glasses. He held his glass to the light. 'Tonight we are celebrating a little English girl's first evening out to dinner.'

Was he teasing her she wondered, already beginning to feel slightly light-headed by the wine. Or was it the influence of convivial surroundings which lifted her spirits? Ramon couldn't have been more sociable and charming, a perfect escort, and she was sorry when the meal came to an end.

After liqueurs he lit a cigarette, and as she

watched the smoke curl slowly upwards, she met his dark questioning eyes through the blue haze. They seemed to search her very soul.

'Must you go now, Vicky?' he asked, as she glanced away.

'Yes, maybe I should leave soon. It was lucky Senora Varela had someone calling and doesn't expect me back too early. I gather her friend stays quite late.'

He rose and came round to move her chair. 'Yes, it was lucky for me too,' he whispered, taking her hand, sending a shiver of delight along her spine, 'and the dress is beautiful. You have been shopping, I see.'

She smiled up at him, happy in the knowledge her trip to Barcelona that afternoon had been worthwhile. 'You remember it, Ramon?'

'Of course.' He laughed. 'You were like a child filled with longing when I saw you that morning.'

During the return journey, soft music played over the radio and she settled back into the luxurious upholstery. Sensing his eyes upon her, she glanced sideways in time to catch his slight frown, before he returned to concentrate on the road ahead, his mouth now set in a firm line. But quite unexpectedly, on the outskirts of Sitges, he pulled off the main road and brought the car to a sudden halt on the grass verge.

Looking at him in surprise, she felt his arm

slide across the back of her seat.

'Do not look so frightened, little English girl,' he said softly. 'I only wish to say thank you for allowing me the pleasure of your company.'

'I enjoyed the evening so much, Ramon,' she answered, a little breathlessly, relaxing again, hardly daring to hope he would repeat the invitation.

He raised her hand to his lips, kissing it gently. 'Gracias, Señorita,' he whispered.

She turned to face him fully, flattered by his charming gesture. 'Oh, I do like the sound of your language, Ramon. It's so musical, so—' she paused, feeling his hand on her hair, untying the velvet bow.

The fair curls fell to her shoulders and he caressed their silky texture. 'So romantic were you going to say, Vicky?'

'Yes, I suppose . . .' she began, suddenly silenced by his lips on hers, gently at first, then firmly, almost hungrily as he took her face in his hands, pulling her towards him. Her heartbeat quickened with shock, and the surprise kept her rigidly upright in her seat until their lips slowly parted. Not daring to open her eyes for a moment, or knowing what to say, she remained motionless until he released her.

'Ah, Vicky!' he exclaimed softly, leaning back in his seat, his eyes still upon her. 'Vicky,' he murmured, almost regretfully, shaking his head slowly and drawing a deep breath. Then, quite abruptly, he turned to face the steering wheel, gripping it tightly as though striving to regain his composure.

Bringing the engine rapidly to life, he revved hard and pulled back on to the road. 'Now you have been kissed by a hot-blooded Spaniard!' he said icily. 'It's what you wanted, isn't it?'

Wordlessly, she stared at him. This unexpected interlude in the journey had left her completely mystified, and her heart thumped wildly.

'What exactly do you mean?' she managed, finally. But, looking at his profile, she saw only the grim set of his mouth, unrelenting, as he accelerated through the darkness. Ramon had retreated into his armour, and drove the remainder of the journey in silence.

It was only minutes at this speedy pace before they were back by the station where he politely wished her goodnight. Yet, walking quickly down the narrow street, she was convinced he watched her, and at the corner, she turned to see him standing under the light of a street lamp.

Perturbed by his unexpected embrace, she delayed the moment of facing Senora Varela by going immediately to her own room, needing time to calm the wild pounding of her heart. The touch of his lips lingered. No one had ever kissed her as Ramon had done. Even

Mark didn't cause her pulses to race this way, but he had completely slipped her mind this evening.

On Sunday, Mark contacted her by phone, saying he had tickets for an orchestral concert the following evening. 'You did say you would be free, Vicky?'

'Yes, thank you, I'd love to go,' she agreed, attempting to sound enthusiastic. But with Friday evening still playing on her mind it was difficult for her to muster a great deal of enthusiasm.

'You're not upset because I'm away on business, are you, darling? I'll make up for it, I promise. An early dinner then, Vicky. I'll call at six-thirty.'

Agreeing to his suggestion, she replaced the receiver and returned to Senora Varela to ensure her staying out a little later met with her approval.

The senora had good news to impart. 'Paul tells me he is employing new staff,' she told Vicky, 'and soon I shall be in my villa again. I have urged him continually and cannot understand the reason for such delay.'

'I'm pleased,' Vicky murmured, wondering how imminent was this move to the villa, and what kind of a man would she find Doctor Paul Varela to be?

CHAPTER SIX

Impatient to reach Barcelona the following morning, Vicky plucked up enough courage to drive Senora Varela to the clinic in the little Citroen, but by the time she reached the doctor's practice, her apprehension mounted over the prospect of coming face to face with Ramon.

Disappointed to find him looking subdued and rather anxious, returning her smile only briefly, her heart sank. Had he regretted that kiss? Had he regretted the evening altogether?

'You did expect me to call this morning?' she queried, with a nervous smile. 'If you're too busy, don't worry—'

'Vicky, please,' he silenced her. 'I must apologise to you. I am sorry for what happened on Friday evening. I should not have taken advantage—'

'Oh, Ramon.' She was blushing now. 'Really, it was a lovely evening.'

'You do not mind being kissed by a man who is almost a stranger to you?'

His voice was harsh, his expression stern, cutting into her deeply, almost as if he had slapped her face.

'You're not a complete stranger,' she declared. 'We are colleagues, but if you'd rather not see me again . . . '

'No, Vicky,' he interrupted quickly, apparently satisfied by her reaction. 'I have promised to show you this city, and I shall do so. This morning we will visit Montjuich by car. From there, you can look over Barcelona.'

They got into the car and he drove until they came to the foot of Montjuich. Further up the grassy slopes of the mountain, they strolled between flower beds and statues which were scattered amongst the trees, finally reaching the Miramar side where she had a splendid view of the city and port.

Standing beside him, shading her eyes, she took in the lovely sight. 'It's a marvellous view. And from here it's hard to believe the city is such a turmoil of traffic and noise. I'm so pleased you brought me, Ramon.'

She turned in her enthusiasm to find he was looking at her intently. He held her gaze for a moment, then with a slightly embarrassed smile, stated huskily, 'Your eyes, they are so very blue,' and proceeded to take a cigarette from his silver case and lit it.

Vicky could do no more than smile at this unexpected compliment, which seemed so foreign to his nature. Confused, she asked herself—what was it that attracted her to the unpredictable temperament of this handsome Catalan? He had kissed her passionately that evening, and now, this morning, had the nerve to chastise her for allowing it!

* * *

The events of the morning served to dampen her desire to spend the evening with Mark, and she had to remind herself that Ramon was purely a colleague, nothing more, so it was ridiculous to let her mind dwell upon him. Determined to push him out of her thoughts, she allowed herself to be swept along in Mark's charming company.

'How beautiful you look this evening,' he complimented, on the drive to Barcelona. 'I shall be the envy of every man.'

Accepting his compliment smilingly, she glanced at him. His easy manner relaxed her. Gone were the tensions she'd experienced earlier, and as he drew up before a restaurant, she looked forward to the remainder of the evening with renewed eagerness.

Over dinner, Mark proved most attentive, coaxing her to try exotic dishes. 'Try it,' he urged, 'if you don't care for it, choose something else!'

'Oh Mark,' she told him, 'you're spoiling me.'

'It makes me happy to see you enjoy yourself, darling. There's no-one else, you know that, don't you?'

'Mark, you can't be sure so soon.'

'I'm very sure, darling. I was attracted to you immediately,' he declared, reaching for her hand, 'you must have noticed?'

She nodded and, slightly overwhelmed by his declaration, attempted to keep the conversation more general as they continued with their meal, before moving on to the theatre.

With chocolates on her lap, and Mark beside her, Vicky settled in her seat to enjoy the music. Occasionally, throughout the concert, his hand would cover hers.

After the final curtain, she declined his offer of a drink in the theatre bar. 'It is a little late,' she reminded him, but seeing his disappointment, agreed to his suggestion of making a short detour by the coast to enable them to stop and talk for a while.

He brought the car to a halt on the coast road where groups of lights indicated villages beside beaches. 'We could take a ride down to the beach one afternoon,' he suggested, 'and perhaps you can show me the villa you'll be moving into soon. I'd love to see the riches it contains. I adore the antiques and paintings these Spanish aristocrats possess.'

'Yes, I believe there are some valuable paintings hanging there, though I know so little about art,' Vicky admitted.

'You would appreciate them if I explained their finer points to you. I'm quite an authority on both antiques and paintings. Haven't you got a key?'

'No, I haven't, and I don't expect to go there until the senora moves.'

'Surely you're allowed to go when you wish? How disappointing for you. See what you can do, Vicky,' he added persuasively. 'Together we could enjoy their treasures so much.'

'I'll try,' she promised, though very unsure of succeeding, remembering the securely locked gates and the heavy wooden door with its large key.

If Ramon held the key for his master, gaining permission would be sure to prove extremely difficult.

'Don't worry. When you do move, perhaps you can invite me and introduce me to your affluent employer. I adore beauty, that's why I'm attracted to you, Vicky. His anyone ever told you what lovely eyes you have?'

'No.' She spoke quietly, denying him the knowledge that only this morning, Ramon had made a similar remark. The memory jolted her, but Mark's further endearments erased the sudden thought.

'But you can guess how I feel about you?' His arm slid about her shoulders, to draw her towards him. 'Hadn't you realised, Vicky? I'm falling in love with you?'

His lips sought hers, kissing them gently.

Surprised but flattered by his declaration, she relaxed in his arms, sure of his sincerity, and she returned his kiss without fear. Tenderly, he caressed her cheek, murmuring softly, 'I love you, Vicky. Meet me again tomorrow, please. I can't bear to be parted from you too long.'

She sighed inwardly. Mark had all the qualities she desired in a man. A steady temperament, thoughtfulness, and a rare charm, but it was Ramon who continued to invade her thoughts, however hard she tried to consider him merely a colleague.

* * *

It was a clinic appointment day once again, and as they descended the marble staircase, Senora Varela paused. 'I want you to do an errand for me, Vicky,' she told her, rather breathlessly, with the effort of walking. 'I want you to go to my son's office, after you leave me at the clinic.'

The request caused Vicky to almost stumble on the last few steps.

'Yes?'

'I will tell you on the journey.' Senora Varela dismissed it for the moment, leaving suspense rising high in Vicky's mind.

It was the opportunity she secretly yearned for, but now the request had been made, she wondered if she could bear to spend time with Ramon when he usually succeeded in leaving her either trembling with suppressed anger, or hopelessly weaving him into her dreams.

As Mark had filled her free evenings during the past week, she had refrained from calling on Ramón when Senora Varela kept her appointments at the clinic. But, even so, she couldn't deny the curious longing which rose strongly within her each time they entered Barcelona.

Impatiently she waited for Senora Varela to continue, but they were almost into the city before she issued further instructions. 'I want you to go to the office and collect something for me. Ask Senor Alvi to get it from the safe for you. It is the flat black box Paul has had placed there for safe keeping.'

With mounting apprehension, Vicky agreed. But, once outside the practice, her nervousness increased so greatly she felt almost unable to continue into the building.

Mounting the stairs, she trembled, her hand clammy on the rail, and swallowing hard she tried to calm the wild beating of her heart. Opening the door, she stood there, silent and motionless until he glanced up. His solemn expression changed quickly to one of unconcealed surprise. 'Vicky!'

'Good morning, Ramon,' she replied calmly. 'Senora Varela asked me to call, otherwise I wouldn't have troubled you.'

'Please sit down.' He indicated a chair. 'I trust you are both quite well?'

'Yes, quite well, thank you.'

Looking at her seriously, Ramon said,' Now you are here, there is something I must tell you.'

He was interrupted by the shrill note of the

telephone bell beside him and, sighing resignedly, he picked up the receiver.

There was a note of urgency in his voice as he replied, then a tone of assurance, and after replacing the receiver, he came towards her with an apologetic smile. 'I am sorry, I must go out immediately.'

Concealing her disappointment, she stood up. 'Of course, Ramon. Oh, I'd almost forgotten. Senora Varela would like the flat black box from the safe. She said her son had it put there for safety.'

For one moment, he appeared completely taken aback, but recovered quickly. 'Ah, yes, certainly. One moment, please.'

Going into his own office, she heard him unlock the safe door, and returning with the box, he slid it into a long envelope.

'Please take great care of this,' he requested, sealing it down.

'Of course. Thank you. Sorry to delay you,' she apologised, walking with him to the outer doorway.

He paused, laying a hand on her arm. 'Can I meet you on Friday evening, Vicky?'

She was rooted to the spot, her heart bubbled over with joy. 'Yes, yes,' she answered, breathlessly, seeing his immediate smile as he turned in the direction of his car.

'Seven, at the station?' he called.

She nodded, as with a wave of his hand, he drove quickly away.

Lost in reverie, it was minutes before she moved to stroll back to the car. This was more than she'd dared to hope for. With a surge of gratitude for Senora Varela, she put the envelope into her bag, suddenly realising there was something strangely familiar about that box. Surely, it was the same one she had seen Ramon put into the safe one morning? There had been visitors to the consulting rooms she recalled; but hadn't they said 'police', or something of that nature? It must be very valuable if the police had brought it from Doctor Varela.

Carefully closing her bag, she drove back to the clinic, bubbling with joy over the forthcoming meeting with Ramon. Thank goodness it would be Senora Forteza's evening to visit.

'Something has made you very happy today,' Senora Varela observed, over lunch. 'I think it is Senor Alvi who brings a sparkle to your eyes,' she continued, smiling mischievously. 'But you did not stay with him for the whole morning?' she queried.

'No, he had to go out rather suddenly.'

'You are to meet him again?'

'Yes,' she replied, hesitantly, then blurted out, 'on Friday evening.'

The lady smiled at her. 'Come upstairs. There is something I wish to show you.'

In her room, Senora Varela took from her bag the envelope Vicky had brought earlier, and opening it carefully, she offered the box for inspection.

There on a velvet pad, lay the most beautiful necklace Vicky had ever seen. A pendant encrusted with deep sapphires and brilliant diamonds. 'It's beautiful,' she whispered.

'It is also valuable, and there was a time when I thought I would not see it again.' Senora Varela gazed into the box, affectionately.

'Had you lost it?' Nicky queried.

'No,' the senora answered, hastily, 'not lost exactly. Tell me, will you wear your blue dress on Friday?'

'Yes, probably. Why do you ask?'

'Then you shall also wear this,' she declared, emphatically. 'I wish you to wear it!'

'Senora Varela, I can't,' Vicky protested. 'It's far too precious.'

The senora held up her hand, silencing any further protests. 'You will take good care of it. It is insured, of course, but that can never replace the sentimental value. It has been with this family for years.'

'Well, thank you,' Vicky yielded. 'It's so kind of you, and I will take extra care, I promise.'

'Good! Soon we shall be returning to my home, maybe next week. I have spoken with Paul and he is making the arrangements, employing new staff. You will like my home, and there you can see all my treasures.

Perhaps you will even consider extending your stay with me?'

'Oh, yes,' Vicky agreed. 'I'd love to.'

'We will decide when we are back in the villa. Then you can be sure you will enjoy life there.'

Delighted by Senora Varela's offer, Vicky realised the contact with Dr Varela's office would continue. Ramon may not be someone who had only drifted into three months of her life after all.

When Friday arrived and it was time to dress for the evening, Senora Varela came to fasten the pendant around Vicky's slim neck. Through the mirror she saw the jewels, perfectly framed in the low neckline, sparkling exquisitely.

'There,' the senora said in a satisfied manner, 'now you look more beautiful than ever. Have a wonderful evening. Go now, I hear Senora Forteza in my room.'

Vicky thanked her once more, and picking up her evening bag, left for the station.

As before, the long black car was already waiting and Ramon greeted her warmly. 'I thought you may like to visit Tarragona this evening,' he suggested. 'It should prove quieter than Barcelona.'

After driving into the town, he parked, suggesting that they walk along the promenade overlooking the sea.

They did this and for a moment, Vicky

paused in the warm, still air, allowing her wrap to slip from her shoulders. 'What a lovely place,' she said, turning towards Ramon.

His eyes dropped to her throat, and with a look of unconcealed amazement, he exclaimed, 'Your pendant!'

'Yes, isn't it beautiful?' She smiled, touching it gently. 'Senora Varela insisted I wear it. It was most kind of her.'

'Senora Varela?' He looked at her almost disbelievingly.

'Yes, she thought it would go well with my dress.'

'It is valuable jewellery,' he observed.

'I know, Ramon, and I promised to take great care of it.'

He looked strangely relieved. 'Come, let us walk to the end of the promenade,' he suggested, taking her arm.

Vicky listened with interest when he told her a little of Tarragona's history as they strolled along.

'It's so beautiful here, Ramon,' Vicky told him. 'I never dreamed Spain had so much to offer.'

'This is only a small part, there is so much more, but,' he added proudly, 'I personally prefer Catalonia.'

'Have you been to the south?'

'Yes, I lived there for a while. It is extremely hot in the summer.'

She laughed. 'I once remember you telling

me so, when I suggested the shutters should always be kept open.'

'You were very new here—I remember, it was when I took you to Villa Barca.'

'Senora Varela is looking forward to returning to her home, Ramon. I hope, for her sake, it will be soon.'

He frowned momentarily, quickly changing the subject by suggesting it was time for dinner.

Seated at the table in the hotel Ramon had chosen, Vicky remarked, 'Senora Varela has asked me to consider extending my service, and it's very tempting.'

'Extend your service?' Ramon asked, his tranquil expression quickly replaced by one of anxiety. 'Vicky, there is something I wish to say. It may not please you, but—'

'Then don't,' she begged, hopeful of retaining the amicable relationship which had prevailed so far this evening, 'don't say anything. I'm enjoying the evening. Let's keep it that way, Ramon, and remain good colleagues.'

He gazed at her thoughtfully. 'If that is what you wish,' he conceded, but she couldn't avoid noticing an uneasiness about him as he held her gaze with dark, haunting eyes.

The dinner and wines were excellent and as the meal progressed, Ramon seemed to discard the discomfort he displayed earlier. 'Whole areas of Tarragona are dedicated to the production of wines,' he informed her, choosing one to accompany their final course.

Thoughtfully, she studied his long fingers as they curled round the stem of his glass, raising it to his lips, and she met his dark eyes under their fringe of thick black lashes.

'What now, my thoughtful colleague?' He smiled, reaching for her hand, and she was confident all was well between them.

Later, they retraced their steps along the cliff road, almost like a balcony above the sea where, pausing by the railings, she tensed as his arm slid gently round her waist. Drawing her closer she felt a shiver of pleasure as his lips brushed her own.

Breaking the gentle contact suddenly, he urged her forward. 'Come,' he said softly, 'come to the garden where we can be alone,' and led her through the laced iron gate, along a path where the foliage grew thickly, until they reached a small sheltered clearing where the scents of many herbs and flowers filled the air.

Her heart beat heavily against her ribs as he paused to gaze down on her. Taking a quick breath, he asked, 'You are happy with our friendship?'

'Yes, very happy,' she replied, though a little uncertain as to why he found it necessary to ask such a question.

'There are certain things I must clarify,' he began, a cool note returning 'and I am certain you will be angry, but—'

'Ramon,' she pleaded, turning away, unable to bear this sharp change of manner, 'please, don't, not now, unless you regret asking me out this evening? If so, we'll go. There's no need to make an issue of it.'

'Vicky, please!' He gripped her wrist, pulling her to him, impatiently. 'No, I do not regret bringing you here.'

'Then why? You keep changing your attitude so suddenly, and we were having such a pleasant evening, until . . .'

'Ah, Vicky.' There was a distinct catch in his voice as he drew her close, his arms tightening around her, then he buried his face in her hair.

'I don't understand you,' she cried easing away, resisting the temptation to remain in his embrace. 'I really don't!'

'Is my manner so strange?' he queried, and she could sense his piercing gaze.

'Strange? No, temperamental,' she returned, with a lift of her chin.

'I do not have the cold blood of the English running through my veins,' he retorted, before his hand grasped her hair and his lips came down on hers with a ferocity she didn't expect.

Her heart pounded violently as she struggled against his grip, but he held her, pulling her against his firm muscular body, and she knew it was useless to expect to gain freedom from his strength.

Quite suddenly, he thrust her away from

him. 'Vicky, forgive me, I go too far! There are other matters which should have been dealt with first. Matters which trouble me. But now I must take you back. Come.' He smoothed her hair and dropped a light kiss on her forehead. 'Let us return to the car. You will call on me?'

Shakily, she walked beside him over the short distance, her mind in turmoil. Never before had she experienced such a desire to be embraced so passionately.

CHAPTER SEVEN

Grateful for Mark's business appointments over the weekend, Vicky's moments of solitude had been spent happily thinking of Ramon and now, as the week began, her impatience to reach Barcelona increased with each passing minute. Wearing a pale blue cotton dress, part of her newly acquired wardrobe, purchased from the generous salary, she was ready well before it was time to start the journey.

'You are to visit Senor Alvi this morning?' Senora Varela guessed, with a shrewd smile. 'He should feel very honoured. You look very pretty today.'

'Yes, I am, and thank you,' Vicky murmured, trying to retain an air of calmness and quell the excitement rising within her.

'Then I will not keep you waiting. I can

sense your impatience.' She smiled, and allowing Vicky to take her arm, proceeded towards the stairway, down to the waiting car.

After leaving Senora Varela in the capable hands of Professor Forteza, Vicky drove into town and, with a light heart, stepped quickly up the wide staircase. This morning the handle didn't give to her turn. She knocked hard, bruising her knuckles on the heavy wooden door. There wasn't a sound from within.

How could Ramon be away? It was only two days since they were together and he hadn't mentioned anything then. Unless—was that what he'd wanted to tell her?

Back outside, Vicky realised that Ramon may possibly return to his office later in the morning. He had expected her to call today, and it was a little early to go back to the clinic. She decided the local shops would fill her time. Her thoughts were interrupted when she realised someone hailed her from the far side of the main road and, shading her eyes, she saw it was Mark.

'Good morning, Vicky,' he called, as he made his way over the crossing.

'Hello, Mark, this is a coincidence.'

'I saw you from that bar.' He pointed across the road. 'Come on, have coffee with me.'

She accepted, knowing it would leave her time to call back at the office before returning to the clinic. Soon she found herself sitting in the window-seat of the cosy little bar, sipping strong coffee.

Mark, obviously delighted to see her so unexpectedly, asked if she would meet him again that evening, and rather than disappoint him, she agreed.

Conversation with Mark was easy and relaxed, but Vicky began to find it hard to keep her concentration, wondering again about the locked office. She smiled and nodded in the right places, but let her eyes wander towards the window and the thick stream of traffic passing by.

Suddenly, without looking up, she was aware of someone standing just outside, facing her, and lifting her gaze she saw the tall dark figure, saw the icy look on his face before he quickly turned away. It was Ramon, and at the piercing look he shot her, she froze, her eyes fixed upon him as he crossed the road to go along the narrow street opposite.

'Vicky, what's the matter? You're not even listening, darling.'

'Sorry, Mark, I'll have to go. I have an appointment to keep, and I didn't realise it was so late.'

'I'll see you across the road,' he insisted, brushing aside her protests, and taking her arm, he guided her through the traffic.

By the doorway of the practice she bade him goodbye, flustered by his presence. 'I really must hurry, Mark.'

He followed her into the hallway, saying,

'And you must call in the bar again next time you're here.'

'Yes, Mark,' she said hastily. 'I'll call another day,' and as she walked towards the stairs, looking upwards, she glimpsed a dark figure moving swiftly out of sight along the landing above.

* * *

With rising trepidation, Vicky took hold of the large door handle, and this time it yielded to her turn. From the reception area she caught sight of Ramon standing beside the desk, his back turned towards her.

'Hello, Ramon. I didn't expect to see you. I thought you were away.'

He turned sharply, allowing her full view of the anger which blazed in his eyes. 'Obviously. And, considering you thought I was away, it did not take you very long to find another companion, did it?'

'Ramon,' she cried, startled by the vehemence of his tone. 'Mark travelled with me on the plane. We are acquainted,' she added defensively, 'but I met him quite by accident today, and . . .'

'And you will meet him again in the bar?' he interrupted, sarcastically. 'Apparently you think nothing of forming such casual relationships, Miss Hurst.'

'At least he is more pleasant than you are

this morning,' she retorted, 'and I did call here first, but you weren't in.'

'And so soon you have found a replacement for me,' came his sarcastic rejoinder. 'I hope for your sake he is as familiar with this city as I am, or perhaps his interest does not only lie in the beautiful buildings of Barcelona?' he finished.

'How dare you!' she exclaimed, indignantly. 'Last Friday you were so different,' she added confusedly, 'why do you change like this?'

He smiled ironically. 'Last Friday I was a fool, but I certainly do not intend to repeat myself after what I see of your behaviour this morning.'

'My behaviour? What about your advances that evening in Tarragona?'

'Do not forget you responded,' he reminded her reproachfully, his dark brows forming a straight line above eyes shining in anger.

'Oh—I—I hate you! And if I want to meet anyone in a bar, I shall do so,' she declared, with a toss of her golden curls.

He glared at her, his eyes hard and calculating, before stating, with infuriating calmness, 'This morning I am rather busy and,' he glanced at his watch, 'I have an appointment very soon. You will excuse me?' he said coldly, dismissing her.

A flush rose to her cheeks, but pride would not allow her to let him guess how hurt and disappointed she felt. With tears filling her eyes, she turned towards the doorway. 'Of course. Goodbye, Ramon,' she replied, stifling the sob which rose to her throat.

Driving back to the clinic, she sought to find an excuse for Ramon's behaviour. Was he jealous? Considering he'd only heard the latter part of Mark's conversation with her, his behaviour was extremely unreasonable. His temper matched his passion—both were unyielding. What ridiculous notion had given her the idea Ramon could ever become more than just a colleague!

At the clinic, she found Senora Valera brimming over with delight.

'Paul telephoned me here, only minutes ago,' she informed Vicky. 'Maybe we shall move home tomorrow, or the following day, though he insists there is no need for a nurse at the villa when he returns. But I have demanded of him that he does as I wish,' she declared, clasping Vicky's hand warmly. 'With you for company, I feel so much better. You will stay?'

* * *

Vicky prepared to meet Mark later that evening. Perhaps she should give more regard to her friendship with him, and sever her thoughts from Ramon completely.

Mark was earlier than she expected, and dressed more formally than was usual for their mid-week dinner dates.

'Oh, are you thinking of going somewhere else?' she asked, eyeing his dinner jacket.

'Sorry, darling, I've got a pressing business appointment over drinks later. Going to have to leave you a little earlier than usual. I could take you with me but it's purely an all male occasion, you'd be bored.'

'It's all right, Mark, I understand.'

'How considerate you are, Vicky, just the sort of girl a chap needs behind him when he's going to the top. I'll see you tomorrow though?'

'Well, I'm not sure, we may be moving to the villa very soon. Can I let you know?'

'Of course, Vicky, and when you do move, don't forget I want that invitation. By the way, I managed to get tickets for the theatre on Friday. You will be able to go?'

'I expect so Mark, thank you.'

Throughout dinner, his eyes hardly left her, and with a look of concern, he remarked, 'You're quiet tonight, Vicky, is anything the matter?'

'No, I'm just a little tired, that's all.'

'You must be working too hard, my dear. I won't keep you. You should have an early night.'

After Mark left for his appointment, Vicky, knowing Senora Varela had company, decided a drive would suit her mood, and went to start her car. The evening air was warm and the narrow streets were filled with strolling people. She gave in to an urge to continue out of town towards the lonely winding road which led to Villa Barca. In the growing darkness, she looked ahead to where the villa stood and felt certain she saw a light go off in one of the windows. Assuming the staff were already installed, she turned the little car in the dusty road and pulled on to the grass verge, winding down the window. Deep in thought, she gazed over the silver flecked water, when a tremendous sense of desolation enveloped her. She was alone with only bewildering thoughts of Ramon's anger going through her mind.

Turning her tear-filled eyes from the sea, she blinked at the sudden brightness of headlights, reflected in the rear-view mirror. The car screeched to a halt behind her, a door slammed, footsteps came closer and quickly she wound up the window and pressed the door catch.

Her heart lurched as the door handle beside her rattled and a voice demanded, 'Open the door!'

With trembling fingers she pulled back the catch. 'Oh, it's you.'

'What are you doing here at this time of night? And what of Senora Varela? How dare you leave her alone!' His voice was harsh. 'You should be with her, not driving alone like this, at night.'

'How dare you!' she snapped, anger rising.

'You have no authority to question me. What I choose to do is no concern of yours, so attend to your own side of Doctor Varela's business, and I'll attend to mine'

Pulling the door shut with a bang, she started the engine and tore off, up the narrow dusty road, at high speed, leaving him standing there.

On reaching the hotel, she found Senora Varela and her friend sitting having a chat. She hoped they wouldn't notice any signs of her recent tears.

'Are you well?' Senora Varela asked a little later after she had joined them.

'Just a little tired,' Vicky answered guardedly. 'It's nothing, really.'

'Maybe the change of climate has affected you, or possibly the food. I will ask my son when he telephones. He will prescribe something for you.'

'Oh no, I'll be all right,' Vicky declined, knowing no doctor could cure her of this ailment. There was no prescription for heartbreak!

'Listen, Vicky, I have news for you. We shall leave here tomorrow, but,' Senora Varela raised her hands despairingly, 'Paul may not return to the villa immediately. He says he has been delayed. He is so difficult and strong willed, but,' she added, indulgently, 'he is my son, what can one do?'

'But he has recovered now. That is the most

important thing,' Senora Forteza reminded her, comfortingly, 'and the trouble is over.'

'Yes, yes, I know,' Senora Varela agreed, glancing sharply in Vicky's direction.

Vicky noticed her glance. What had the trouble been, she wondered? Had Doctor Varela suffered an accident? It seemed strange his mother appeared so reluctant to discuss it.

'You will come to my home on Friday?' the senora continued. 'It will be wonderful to be back again.'

'Of course,' Senora Forteza assured, as she rose to embrace her friend. 'I shall call as usual.'

'Then may I ask if it will be convenient for me to go out on Friday?' Vicky broke in, hopeful that an evening at the theatre would help erase some of her unhappiness.

Immediately the thought had passed through her mind, she felt a pang of guilt. Dear Mark. She should never have considered him second best, as a foil for her disappointment over Ramon. That arrogant Catalan just wasn't worth all the heartache he caused her to suffer.

'Of course,' the senora enthused. 'You will enjoy our famous theatre. Where did you go this evening? Anywhere special?'

'I had a quiet drive,' Vicky answered slowly. 'I was thinking of what we need to pack before we leave for the villa—'

'Ah, that reminds me, on Wednesday I wish

you to call in at the office. There are other keys to collect.'

Vicky's heart turned over. 'Oh, I can't, I mean, there won't be time with moving and all that.'

'Of course there will be time. We shall go to the clinic as usual,' Senora Varela declared.

After a restless night, Vicky had little time to think of her own unhappiness. There was the final packing to do and she was kept busy.

With the help of the proprietor, she squeezed their luggage into the boot of the car while Senora Varela waited in the front. They made their way to the villa, and determined not to allow Ramon to enter her thoughts, Vicky kept her eyes averted from the spot where she had parked the previous evening.

On reaching the villa, she swung the heavy iron gates inwards and drove round to the main door, where the staff waited, and formal greetings were exchanged.

As Senora Varela went indoors with Tina, the housekeeper, Vicky approached the couple outside.

The young man said, 'I am the chef, José.' And, turning to the dark-haired young woman beside him added, 'This is Isabella, she help.'

Vicky extending her hand, greeting them, then asked, 'Could you help me with the luggage, please?'

'We come from Granada,' Jose told her as he unloaded the cases. 'This very nice house, and the doctor is a good man. Senora Varela, she is okay?'

'You have met the doctor?' Vicky asked in surprise.

'Yes, he come for three days.'

Vicky wondered if Senora Varela was aware her son had been here. It seemed strange he hadn't called at the Romantic.

Slowly, following Senora Varela into each room on her tour of inspection, Vicky saw the dust sheets had been removed, revealing rich upholstery, highly polished woodwork and, hanging on the plain walls, were many beautiful paintings. The whole atmosphere spelled quality.

'You like my home?' Senora Varela asked, as they climbed the wide staircase.

Vicky swallowed hard, as a lump rose in her throat. 'It's beautiful,' she said sincerely. 'I'm lucky to have such a lovely place in which to live.'

'While you are here it is your home, and,' Senora Varela paused, 'I hope it will be, for a long time.'

* * *

'Do not forget to call at the office for the keys,' Senora Varela reminded Vicky as they pulled into the clinic driveway.

Vicky nodded, though doubtful as to her ability to face the ordeal. But on reaching the consulting rooms, she found Ramon looking expectantly towards the doorway.

He came forward quickly, indicating a chair by his desk, and asking her to be seated. 'Before we go any further, I wish to apologise to you for my sharp words the last evening we met so unexpectedly. Since then, I have learned Senora Varela had company, and you had given her the opportunity to speak with her guest privately. I do hope you will forgive me. This also leads me to explain how I may appear to be so knowledgeable of the Varela family's affairs. I tried to tell you the last time, but now it has become most necessary that I should explain.'

'Just a moment,' she interrupted, his composed and precise manner infuriating her. 'Do you think that merely by a simple apology you put everything to rights? You calmly apologise for your rudeness in the evening, but what about the morning? You were extremely uncivil to me then.'

'You must admit I had good reason,' he replied confidently.

'Nonsense,' she replied. 'I did offer to explain on both occasions, but you were so autocratic I couldn't get a word in.'

He smiled wryly, and moved round the desk to sit in the large swivel chair behind. 'It is most difficult this explanation,' he began, giving her a brief smile, 'but I hope you will try to understand,' he continued, only to be interrupted by the shrill bell of the telephone on his desk. Sighing with annoyance, he picked up the receiver.

She saw a look of intense displeasure cross his face and the muscles of his jaw tensed. 'Who is this?' he said finally, in English. There was a long pause before he replied to the caller with a vehemence that made Vicky wince. 'Most certainly not. Do not call this number again!'

With anger blazing on his face, Ramon banged the receiver on to its rest and stood up.

'Whatever is the matter, Ramon?' Vicky asked.

'You should not encourage a young man, then disappoint him, Miss Hurst,' he said furiously. 'Such behaviour is not acceptable here.'

'Whatever are you talking about?' she gasped. 'I don't know what you mean.'

'Then let me enlighten you,' he offered, harshly. 'This friend of yours—he has the audacity to telephone me after trying to reach you at the hotel.'

'Do you mean Mark?'

'The very same, yes.'

'I haven't encouraged him to telephone me here, please believe me.'

'Believe you,' he retorted. 'This man flippantly tells me you had arranged to meet him for coffee this morning, but have not kept the appointment. How can I believe you?'

'I didn't make a definite arrangement, Ramon, really I didn't. It was only a casual remark—'

'Do you think I am a fool?' he asked. 'Do you think I do not know. You are just the same! Go, he is waiting for you in the bar!'

She stood up, meeting his hard stare. 'All right, I will, but don't expect me ever to come here again. I only came for the keys!'

He pushed them across the desk. 'Please leave me,' he snapped, turning away.

She drove off with Ramon's bitter words ringing in her ears and tears streaming down her face, past the bar where Mark waited. She couldn't possibly face him now, not this morning. Surely his phone call didn't warrant such aggression on the part of Ramon?

There was a telephone call for Senora Varela after they returned from the clinic. Tina brought the instrument to the luncheon table, and a lengthy conversation followed, then Vicky observed a smile on the senora's face.

'I have told a small lie.' She chuckled, after replacing the receiver. 'Paul says there is no reason for him to return here while I have a nurse, so I told him you were flying home next week.'

'Senora Varela!' Vicky exclaimed. 'What will he say when he finds me here?'

'That does not matter, I know he will like you but first I must persuade him to come home, then we shall give him the big surprise!'

Vicky had mixed feelings over Doctor Varela's surprise and wondered anxiously what kind of reception she would receive from him.

The following day, on her way to collect Senora Varela's breakfast tray, Vicky picked up the post and, sorting through them, she was surprised to see a typewritten envelope addressed to herself. Her heart leapt when she saw the Barcelona postmark.

With trembling fingers she slit open the envelope, to find a letter in Ramon's bold hand-writing, which read, '*Vicky, I apologise for my angry words of yesterday. I understand you are leaving, and do not wish we should part company on such bad terms. I had no right to censure your friendships, or criticise, but as you're leaving, my explanation is not necessary. I would prefer to give you this apology personally, and regret I am unable to do so. I wish you a safe journey to England and hope that you will forgive me. Sincerely, Ramon.*'

Vicky's lip trembled. What did Ramon and Doctor Varela discuss so personally for him to have learned she was soon to leave—or so the doctor thought? And what would his explanation have been? Could it be he was promised to another? Betrothed to a young lady of good local family—a Catalan no doubt, and that was what he'd wanted to explain so many times? Perhaps it would be wiser if she did choose to leave soon, and forget him. If Ramon was bound by a promise, there was nothing she could do.

CHAPTER EIGHT

He anticipated visit to the theatre had done nothing towards lifting her spirits, and without a great deal of enthusiasm, Vicky drove into Barcelona to meet Mark.

They reached their seats in time to see the musicians position themselves before tuning their instruments, and she gazed around the magnificent hall, decorated lavishly in gold and red, with its many private boxes, treasured by the families who visited regularly.

Her attention returned to the platform as applause rose for the lead violinist, and again as the conductor took his place on the dais, bringing a sudden hush to the theatre. As he brought down his baton, the concert began and Vicky was lost in the music of Wagner.

After the final curtain, as the applause died away and the lights came up again, she turned to Mark. 'That was wonderful, I'm so glad—' she began, but hesitated, noticing the man seated in front of Mark, seeing the pallor of his face and the way he clutched his chest as he uttered a deep moan. The man appeared extremely ill, and the lady beside him began to show signs of alarm.

Quickly, Vicky was on her feet, cradling the

man's head in her arm as she felt for his pulse, noticing the perspiration standing on his brow; his condition seemed grave. She pleaded with Mark to get help. 'There may be a doctor in the audience, please hurry!'

Someone rushed up the aisle towards them, and she heard Mark speak rapidly, with a sense of urgency in his tone.

'I have asked for a doctor,' Mark informed her.

Feeling relieved help would soon be at hand, Vicky loosened the man's collar and tie. His breathing was difficult, almost inaudible as she bent closer, when his eyelids flickered and closed. Promptly, she heard footsteps coming swiftly along the aisle and, glancing up, saw the manager. Another man followed close at his heels; hopefully this would be the doctor.

Raising her eyes to the newcomer, she suddenly froze. There stood Ramon.

Only the urgency of the situation enabled her to keep calm. 'Have you found a doctor?' she entreated, but Ramon didn't answer. Instead, he demanded the immediate area be cleared as he advanced rapidly towards the ailing man.

'Come, help me,' he commanded, lowering the man to the floor.

She was amazed by the way he handled the situation, knowing it to be serious, but why didn't he listen to her? There must be a doctor somewhere near!

'Ramon,' she said, sharply, 'he's had an arrest, a heart attack, we . . .'

'The doctor's here, darling,' Mark intervened, 'so you needn't—'

'Start breathing,' Ramon ordered, glaring at her, 'resuscitate him,' and she watched him bring his hand down in a heavy blow on the man's chest.

Vicky quickly tilted the sick man's head back, before commencing to breathe rhythmically, hopefully exhaling life-giving air from her own body into his.

During this crisis, although Vicky's mind reeled with shock, she succeeded in keeping up the rhythm. She shot a glance at Ramon, his expression grave, his hands massaging, working to bring back life to the still body. As a team they continued, unconscious of time, until almost exhausted, but finally rewarded by a faint pulse and a gasp. The man now breathed independently, and his heart battled on weakly.

As the ambulancemen arrived, Ramon sat back on his heels, breathing heavily. 'Relax a moment,' he advised, adding quietly, 'I think he will survive.'

Stunned and exhausted, Vicky stared at him, unable to utter a word. Even while she had helped deal with this emergency, her mind had been in turmoil. Doctor Varela! So that was the reason for his strange behaviour, but why? She could never forgive him this lie, or the way he had treated her.

With the patient on a stretcher, Ramon stood up and, holding the man's pulse, proposed, 'We had better accompany him to the hospital.' And to Mark he directed, 'I suggest you do not wait. My apologies for disorganising your evening, but I need the help of your companion.'

Mark smiled. 'I understand. Ring me, Vicky, will you?'

Vicky nodded and followed the stretcher in silence, too stunned to do otherwise, knowing her services may yet be necessary.

The patient held on to life throughout the journey, and on reaching the hospital, Ramon went with him into the curtained cubicle which had been prepared.

Sitting on a hard chair in the corridor, Vicky waited until the activity behind the curtain ceased. Eventually a nurse pushed it aside, allowing Ramon to emerge, followed by another doctor. The concern on their faces had lessened and, happily, she assumed the man's life was out of danger.

As Ramon walked towards her, a surge of anger rose strongly within her and she turned away. Walking down the long corridor, she was aware of him close behind her.

'Vicky, listen to me. You helped me to save a man's life, do you realise that? You are an excellent nurse.'

She looked back at him, her face flushed

with anger. 'How could you?'

'Come,' he said, taking her arm, 'we cannot talk here. I will take you back to the villa.'

Choosing to ignore the hand he offered, she shrugged him away and walked on, furious over having no alternative.

Inside his car, she faced him, coldly. 'I am sorry you have the trouble of taking me to Sitges. I can assure you I shall not be a further nuisance to you senor, whatever your name is!'

She had never felt so humiliated. How could he just sit there looking at her, silently—his eyes anxious, searching—her employer!

'Vicky, please, do not be so angry. I have tried to tell you many times.'

'Not be angry,' she shouted. 'You led me to believe you are his—your secretary, and ask me out, take me to dinner and, and—'

'And kiss you?' He took her hands, gripping them firmly. 'Listen to me, Vicky. Remember, it was you who presumed I was Senor Alvi on our first meeting in my office, though I must admit, for a certain reason I allowed you to. I agree, you were misled, but then it did not matter who I was. Only when we began to meet more regularly did it become important, but how was I to tell you? I knew you would be hurt!'

'I am and I hate you for it! What an underhand way to discover what I am like, both professionally and socially.'

'Please, I do not wish us to part company

with such feelings of animosity. You must not go away with bitterness and anger in your heart. Are you not due to fly tomorrow?'

'Oh, no.' She remembered his mother had told him this. 'I was, but Senora Varela wishes me to stay a little longer, and I gather you objected, now I realise why. You wouldn't want to know me once you returned to the villa. A man in your position, escorting his mother's nurse—how socially degrading for you.' With tears brimming in her eyes, she added bitterly, 'I would be just another of your servants.'

'Vicky,' he snapped, impatiently, 'that is not so.'

'What about the last companion, whom you dismissed so suddenly?' she rejoined sharply.

'I do not wish to discuss her,' he told her firmly. 'It is no concern of yours, but I do prefer you should remain.'

'How can I stay now? I can't possibly complete three months'

'Did you not once declare you would never let a patient down? And, do remember, you signed a contract.'

'Doctor Varela,' she began, coolly releasing herself from his firm grip, 'I am your employee, and if you insist on holding me to that contract, then I shall endeavour to continue with my duties as before, though I don't doubt you will have found fault with them during your amateur attempts at impersonation.'

'Vicky,' he exclaimed, crossly. 'My mother speaks extremely highly of your services, and I also know you have cared for her well. But if it distresses you so greatly to be in my company,' he added, 'I shall endeavour to keep my distance. And also,' he continued, sarcasm edging his words, 'this English gentleman you associate with—in my opinion, he is not a suitable escort.'

'You mean Mark Gildner,' she said, indignantly. 'You may be my employer but it doesn't give you the right to choose my friends and, come to think of it, I don't recall Mark telling me any untruths.'

'Do not let me find this young man near my house, ever!' he told her severely, and he ignored any further protests by starting the car rapidly and accelerating out of the grounds into the quiet streets.

Sleep evaded her for the remainder of the night, as thoughts of the crisis in the theatre, mingled with the shock of meeting Ramon in unexpected circumstances cascaded through her mind.

The moment she arrived back at the villa had been almost unbearable. Senora Forteza was still there, enthusing over the competent way they had dealt with the situation, and Senora Varela, excited over the unexpected arrival of her son, wished them to relate the whole sequence of events again. 'Now you have met my son,' she'd declared happily, turning to Vicky who hadn't the heart to mention the fact she had known him from the beginning, but as Senor Alvi.

Now, this morning, as she dressed, the firing of a car engine came clearly from outside and, looking down through the partly open shutters, she saw the long black car turn towards the gateway and caught a glimpse of Ramon looking up at the window. It hadn't occurred to her he would stay at the villa overnight. She had been too full of her own distress to consider it. But, of course, there was no reason for him to stay away now, no more need for him to conceal his identity.

'Paul has already left for the city,' Senora Varela announced, as Vicky joined her for breakfast, 'so he is unable to join us.'

Hearing him called Paul seemed strange. Ramon was someone who didn't exist in her life any more. Ramon had been a dream.

As the days went by, she saw little of Ramon, and when they did meet, it was usually in his mother's company. He was polite, casually passing the time of day, but no more.

For the past week, meetings with Mark had been shortened, and they usually dined in a local hotel or drove into the country in his white sports car. Mark possessed so many good qualities; he was charming and thoughtful, but each time he kissed her, there was none of the aching desire which had surged through her body as when Ramon had pressed his lips to hers.

She sighed. A whole week had passed since that unforgettable evening in the theatre and she had tossed and turned through many sleepless hours, anxiously searching for an answer. Tonight was no exception, the hollow single chime of the hall clock echoed up the wide staircase. She felt utterly exhausted—maybe a hot drink would help to relax her tired body.

She tiptoed down the stairs and, crossing the tiled hall, noticed a chink of light coming from under the lounge door. Thinking Tina must have forgotten to switch it off when they left the room earlier, she opened the door. About to put her hand on the switch, she suddenly realised there was someone in the room.

A ring of grey smoke curled upwards from the settee, and a dark head rose. Surprise glued her to the spot. It was Ramon—she had missed hearing the familiar crunch of his car tyres on the driveway.

'Oh—I'm sorry,' she wavered. 'I thought the light had been left on by mistake.'

'Vicky, don't go.' His tone was coaxing, and her body tensed.

'It's very late, I must—'

'Come here, Vicky,' he directed crisply, as he rose. 'Close the door.'

She closed the door and faced him, feeling extremely vulnerable. 'Yes, doctor, what is it?'

'Vicky, we must not continue this way, it is impossible. Can we not at least be good friends?' His eyes held pleading, and her heart beat faster at his persuasive tone. 'I will not believe you hate me so much,' he declared angrily. 'Or,' he asked, 'do your affections still lie with Mark Gildner?'

'That is my business,' she retorted. 'I am sorry,' she added firmly, 'we have nothing to discuss, unless there is anything you wish to say as my employer.'

Without giving him a chance to continue she left the room quickly, rushing upstairs to the safety of her own room. Inside, she leant against the door, her heart pounding hard. She had succeeded, remained cool and distant, not succumbed to his appeal, but now derived no pleasure from her success.

Flinging herself on the bed, her shoulders heaving, and tears running freely down her cheeks, she knew the following weeks were going to be hard to endure.

CHAPTER NINE

After lunch, the following day, Ramon returned to the villa early and sought Vicky out as she prepared Senora Varela for her afternoon rest. 'Vicky, may I have a word with you?' he asked, after dropping a light kiss on his mother's cheek.

'Certainly, doctor,' She managed a brief smile as she plumped up the cushions.

'My new patient, the cardiac arrest, he is improving. I thought you would wish to know.'

'Yes, I had wondered, and I am so pleased. He will recover?'

'Yes, I am sure, and,' he added hesitantly, 'he wishes to thank you personally. This morning, when I called at the hospital, he begged me to ask you this favour. He will be hospitalised for a considerable time but requests to meet you before you leave for England.'

He looked at her expectantly, causing a stab of guilt. Although she had been anxious about the sick man, because of her pride, she had made no effort to inquire of Ramon about his patient's health.

'Yes, of course I will visit him but not to be thanked. It will be a pleasure to see him well again. I'm sorry, I should have asked you before.'

'And I could have told you,' he replied quietly. 'If you wish, I will drive you to the hospital this afternoon.'

'Thank you, but I don't want to trouble you—' She broke off as his eyes narrowed and quickly added, 'Well, if it isn't inconvenient, thank you for your offer.'

When they arrived at the hospital, they entered a private room where, at the bedside,

Ramon translated his patient's words of thanks.

Lying there, with gratitude shining from his eyes, he reached for Vicky's hand. She took it gently, asking Ramon to tell him she had been only too happy to help. 'And please convey my good wishes for his speedy recovery, Ramon.'

Outside again, Ramon asked her to wait in the car. He returned soon, carrying flowers, which he said, his patient had asked him to purchase, as a token of gratitude.

A lump rose in Vicky's throat as she took the red carnations and met Ramon's warm smile. 'How kind. Thank you for choosing them. Perhaps you will give him my thanks when you next visit?'

He didn't reply, but thrust a small parcel on to her lap. 'Also for your help—I am grateful—but please open it later,' he requested, starting the engine quickly, and turning the car in the direction of Sitges.

She turned, but he was looking straight ahead, his profile expressionless. 'Thank you, but I didn't expect anything, and I can't really accept this.'

'Please, you must accept this small token of my gratitude,' he entreated, unsmilingly.

Feeling it would be ungracious not to, she murmured her thanks again. 'It really is most kind of you. It will be something to remind me of Spain.'

'Remind you?'

'Yes, a souvenir to take home.'
'Home?' he asked quickly. 'I understood you had agreed to extend your time here? Why have you changed your mind?'
'Why? Ramon, you ask why!' she cried. 'You know I can't stay here, not now.'
'You were happy with me before, Vicky?'
'Yes,' she admitted, feeling her colour rise. 'But tell me something, why did you impersonate your own secretary?'
'My secretary had to go away suddenly, for an indefinite period, so I took on his work also, rather than seek a replacement. I had planned to tell you at a suitable time but on each opportunity, something happened to prevent it. Along came the night of the concert; you know what happened then?'
'How could I forget? And you can't even offer a reasonable explanation.'
'I notice you still call me Ramon,' he replied, with a quizzical smile. 'At the time I suppose I wanted to escape reality and not get hurt. It was a way of evading the questions when I had to cancel the conference—'
'Ramon, this is ridiculous. I don't intend suffering further distress by staying here. I must leave as soon as possible!'

* * *

She opened the little parcel at bedtime, and, to her surprise, she found a beautiful gold bracelet lying in a blue velvet box. It was a gift she could not possibly accept. But Ramon had left by the time Vicky attended to Senora Varela's dressing the following morning.

As Vicky tidied herself before lunch, she heard Tina on the landing outside her room.

'Has the doctor returned?' she called, hopeful of an early opportunity to speak with him.

'Not yet. I expect he will return for dinner,' Tina advised, coming into the room. 'Senora Varela tells me you have been to Barcelona with him to visit his patient,' she continued, pulling her dark curls into place before the mirror. 'How is he?'

'Who?' Vicky asked, absent-mindedly, her glance straying to the vase of red carnations. 'Oh, the patient—yes, he is improving considerably.'

Tina was beside her now, her smile teasing. 'Did Doctor Varela give you those?' she asked, indicating the flowers. 'I am sure he likes you!'

'No, the patient gave them to me,' Vicky explained quickly.

'Red carnations once meant something very special in this house,' Tina remarked. Then, spotting the blue box, asked, 'What have you bought? Can I look?'

Not waiting for consent, she picked it up and lifted the lid, her eyes widening in surprise.

'It was a present for my help with the

gentleman who was ill.'

'It's beautiful! Did the patient give you that?' Tina gasped, as she stared at the delicately carved gold bracelet lying there. But, glancing at Vicky's warm face, she added shrewdly, 'Or was it the doctor?'

'Yes, but I must return it, it's much too valuable.'

'Oh Vicky, you must not do that, it would not be gracious of you. And do you know what it means when a gentleman gives a young lady a bracelet?' Tina laughed, rolling her dark eyes expressively. Ignoring Vicky's curiosity, she continued, 'But he seems so cross when your name is mentioned now. He looks so . . .' She imitated Ramon's supposedly downcast expression.

'I'm sure I don't know why!' Vicky exclaimed, then she smiled at Tina. 'Tell me about the flowers. Why did they once have a special meaning in this house?'

'I should not really speak of this,' Tina replied.

'Why not?'

'The senora forbids it. Please do not ask, Vicky.'

'In that case, I won't press you,' she assured the other girl, noticing Tina's uneasiness.

Still troubled by the quality of Ramon's gift, Vicky delayed her departure from the villa, hoping to have the opportunity to speak with him before it was time to keep her appointment for dinner with Mark. But by seven o'clock, he still hadn't returned.

Mark appeared a little impatient when she joined him. 'Thought you'd got lost, darling. Let's have dinner now. I want to spend a little time alone with you tonight.'

During the meal, he was extremely attentive but impatient to take her for a drive by the coast. And, once in his car, he drove to a secluded spot overlooking the sea then taking her in his arms, whispered words of love.

'Darling, you must know I need you. When can we be married?'

'Married! Oh, Mark, what can I say.'

'Please, darling, say yes. And let me take you home tonight.'

'I don't think it would be wise, not until I've mentioned you first. In any case, I'm not likely to be there much longer, I'm due to return to England in less than two weeks. What shall we do then?'

'We'll be married in England, as soon as possible,' he declared eagerly. 'Oh, Vicky, I do love you so much.'

'But, I haven't . . .'

'You will, darling, you must. I can give you a life of luxury, anything you wish for, and I shall always love you, you know that, don't you?'

'I don't know what to say. Let me have a day or two to think about it, please. I really ought to go now,' she added, realising it was getting quite late.

'Take me back to the villa with you. If the old lady's in bed, no one will ever know, and I'm absolutely dying to see the place.'

'I'm sorry, Mark, I can't, really, Doctor Varela may have returned by now.'

'Who? Doctor Varela did you say?'

'Yes, he was at the theatre that evening, you remember. Do you know him?'

Mark was silent for a moment, then he gave a short laugh. 'Well, in a way, yes. I understand he's one of the richest men in the city. By jove, you certainly picked an affluent employer.'

'I didn't realise it. Are we still going to the theatre on Friday?' she asked, changing the subject.

'Oh, er, yes, I'll let you know about that when I get the tickets.'

Briefly, Mark kissed her and she noticed his manner seemed a little subdued. Much to her relief, his previous urge to visit the villa appeared to be forgotten. As they reached the square where her car was parked, she was surprised when he got out immediately to help her alight.

'I'll ring you soon, Vicky,' he told her.

About to reply, she glanced around her before stepping on to the road, and what she saw caused the words to stick in her throat.

A long black car slid quietly round the corner, and in the light of the well illuminated square, she saw Ramon's hard stare.

Mark pulled away quickly. Once inside her

own little car, Vicky sat a while before driving slowly towards the villa, hoping to ensure Ramon would have retired to his own room before she arrived. Attempting to shrug off the feeling of trepidation which had overcome her, she tried to consider Mark's proposal, but only Ramon's stern features continued to invade her mind throughout the journey.

The hallway was in darkness as she entered, and, about to mount the first step, she froze as a shaft of light caught her.

'Miss Hurst, one moment please.' Ramon stepped aside, indicating her to enter the lounge.

Here, at last, was the opportunity she had sought throughout the day, but by his expression she doubted he was in a suitable mood to accept what may seem an ungracious refusal of his gift.

He quietly closed the door behind her and beckoned her forward to a chair.

'No, thank you, I won't stay,' she declined. 'But I did want to have a word with you about . . .'

'About what?' he asked, in clipped tones. 'I think you owe me many words, particularly ones of explanation.'

He reached for his lighter, and as he flicked it to a flame his eyes never left her face. Drawing on a cigarette deeply, he continued, in a controlled voice, 'I warned you about your choice of companion, yet only this very evening I observe that you continue with this foolishness. He is a most undesirable person, and I forbid you to see this man again. While you are in my house, I am responsible for you, and I demand that you should respect my wishes. Is that quite clear?'

Vicky met his cold stare angrily. 'Doctor Varela, you may be my employer but you are not my guardian! Really it is too much. Mark is a thoroughly honourable man, and he doesn't have your unreasonable temperament. Also, he's very fond of me,' she concluded, turning to leave the room.

'Fond of you,' he retorted, taking her wrist in a vice-like grip and pulling her back to face him. 'You really believe this man loves you?'

'Yes, and why not?' she asked, wrenching herself free and meeting his piercing stare. 'He asked me to marry him.'

'Marry him?' Ramon echoed, in shocked tones. 'You can't marry him!'

'Of course I can! I shall not be here for very much longer, and whatever I choose to do after that will be no concern of yours, Doctor Varela,' Vicky told him, and rushed from the room.

An opportunity to return the bracelet still hadn't presented itself two days later, and on Friday morning she was again dismayed to hear Ramon's car pull out of the drive at a very early hour. Everything seemed to be going wrong, and Mark hadn't telephoned to say if he'd acquired tickets for the theatre that very evening.

After breakfast, deciding to try Mark's number, she was relieved to hear his voice at last.

'Terribly sorry, darling,' he replied, in answer to her query, 'can't get tickets, absolutely sold out.'

'Never mind Mark, we can meet and take a drive by the beach again.'

'Darling, I'm afraid we must call it off tonight, some business has cropped up. Dashed hard luck I know, but I can't get out of it. Must meet this other chap. I'll ring you early next week, Vicky.'

'Yes, Mark, I understand. Please ring soon—' she began, only to hear his receiver drop, closing the line.

'I won't be going out this evening after all,' she informed Senora Varela on returning to remove the breakfast tray. 'My friend has a business appointment.'

Senora Varela folded her newspaper and straightened. 'So you are free this evening, should I need you?'

'Yes, of course, and Senora Forteza will be here, too, I presume?'

'She will,' the Senora agreed, with a slight frown, as she took up the paper once more to stare thoughtfully at the print.

Vicky felt she had been dismissed, and in the adjoining dressing-room she hung the senora's clothes in the wardrobe. Hanging away the final garment, she paused suddenly. The unmistakable sound of tyres crunching over the gravel outside made her cross to the window, and she was in time to see Ramon about to enter the door below. Unaccountably, her heart began to beat a little faster, and in minutes she heard him enter the adjoining room where Senora Varela was. They exchanged greetings in their own tongue before continuing a conversation in lowered tones.

Closing the wardrobe door, Vicky crossed the room to re-enter the lounge. 'I'll attend to the other tasks later,' she said, advancing towards the main door.

'Vicky, one moment,' Senora Varela called, 'my son wishes to speak with you'

Vicky hesitated, her curiosity aroused by Ramon's troubled expression. 'Yes, doctor? I was hoping for the chance of a word with you myself, but perhaps this is not a suitable time?'

'Perhaps it will keep,' he suggested, advancing towards her. 'I must leave soon to attend to one of my patients, but before I go, I wish to extend an invitation to you. I feel it would be wrong of us to allow you to leave Spain without first sampling some of the many delightful customs of this region. Perhaps you will allow me to escort you to a square in Barcelona where we can partake in a dance called the sardana. Also, in the evenings, there's the flamenco,' he continued, unaware of the tremor of shock which ran through her body. 'Anyone who visits this country should not return without first seeing and hearing one of the best known entertainments we have to offer. Surely you have experienced some feelings of interest?'

She stared at him in disbelief for some time before managing a reply. 'You are asking me to go with you?'

'Most certainly,' he replied quietly. 'I extend this invitation in the hope you will accept, if only to furnish yourself with happy memories of Catalonia.'

'Thank you, but really I can't,' she faltered, her cheeks suddenly drained of colour.

'Of course you can,' Senora Varela interrupted, having followed the conversation with interest.' You are free this evening, no?'

'Yes.'

'Then it is settled. Paul will take you into the city where you will see one of the most superb teams of flamenco dancers.'

One glance at Senora Varela's face told Vicky the lady was determined to ensure she accepted the invitation. But how on earth was she to endure an evening in Ramon's company after their recent stormy arguments?

CHAPTER TEN

Vicky found her disappointment over not seeing Mark gradually fading as she dressed for the evening, and now a curious excitement ached within her. Telling herself it was merely suspense over the forthcoming challenge, she slipped on a light silky dress in a delicate shade of pink.

Her eyes lighted on the blue box. Opening it, she gazed down at the gold bracelet. This was hardly the moment to return the gift, but she would mention it.

Descending the staircase, she found Ramon already awaiting her in the hall.

'You are very punctual, and extremely pretty,' he remarked, his gaze flickering over her appraisingly as he ushered her towards the doorway.

Comfortably seated in the luxurious interior of his car, her awareness of him heightened, causing her to tremble at the thought of refusing his gift.

As the car sped down the hill towards the main road, she drew a long, shaky breath before turning to face him. 'Doctor, there's something I must say before we go any further. It's about the bracelet you gave me. I can't possibly accept such a valuable gift. It really was most kind of you, and I don't wish to appear ungracious, but I'd prefer it if you'd allow me to return it to you.' She ran her tongue around her lips, apprehensive as to what change of mood she may induce.

But Ramon merely raised his brows and smiled, saying, 'And, if I should declare such an action ungracious, you would have no alternative but to accept? Please, if you insist on leaving, then keep it, even if it only serves to remind you I am not completely heartless, nor a man to be despised entirely.' Covering her hand with his own, he added, 'This evening must not be spoiled by our disagreements. There is much to do and see which will take your mind off my shortcomings.'

'Then I'll drop the subject for this evening. We can discuss it at some future date, although I have very little time left now.'

'I have a proposition to make,' he offered, gently. 'If you are still of the same mind on the day you depart Sitges, then leave the bracelet behind. Is that not a fair suggestion?'

Vicky nodded and smiled. There was no doubt in her mind; intent on making this an evening to remember, Ramon was determined to keep any tension out of their relationship. It was to be a memorable experience of Spanish tradition which she could recall with pleasure on her return to England.

They pulled up before a night club, and once inside, Ramon exchanged a few words with the manager who signalled the head waiter to escort them to a table in a secluded area of the room.

Once seated, Ramon ordered an aperitif which they sipped by candlelight. The service was excellent, and they were treated with extreme courtesy. Ramon looked most distinguished beside her as he gave the waiter his order.

After dinner, spotlights hit the floor, and, full of excitement and colour, the dancing began. Ramon leaned closer. 'This is the cante chico,' he told her, 'which is popular at the floor shows, but there is also the cante jondo, songs of human drama, life, death, and,' he paused, meeting her eyes searchingly, 'love.'

He continued to hold her gaze, and she was extremely aware of the intensity of her feelings for him, as the guitars throbbed in time with the stamping heels and songs that came from the soul.

Vicky tore her eyes away, to the beautiful dark-haired girl who twirled dramatically, flourishing the bright ruffles of her dress, her hands making expressive movements in the air. The singer rendered a few lines before the hand clapping began, slowly at first, quickening to an amazing speed as the dance progressed. The dancer continued to twirl and gesticulate, keeping her gaze on the arrogant dark man with eyes half closed who poised rigidly beside her, almost as though she flirted with him.

As the dance finished, Vicky applauded enthusiastically and, turning to Ramon, found his eyes still resting upon her, narrowed and thoughtful, as if unaware of his surroundings and the colourful spectacle just performed with its pulsating sounds.

'That was absolutely wonderful, Ramon,' she told him. 'I don't know how they can clap their hands and click their heels so rapidly.'

He smiled at her wide-eyed appreciation. 'They learn to dance at a very early age, and are dedicated to keeping the tradition alive.'

As the flamenco troupe left the floor, the music changed to that of a gently playing trio.

'Shall we dance?' Ramon asked, taking her hand, causing her heart to give the strangest lurch.

Being in his arms once more brought an almost unbearable tingling sensation to her whole being. The feeling within her heightened as he pulled her a little closer, and she felt his chin rest gently against her forehead as they moved slowly round the small floor. But the turmoil in her mind increased. This was purely a social occasion shared with her employer, she reminded herself. Yet, even such a reminder didn't serve to erase the pleasurable ache within her, and an involuntary sigh escaped her as his lips lightly touched her forehead.

'Are you happy here with me?' he whispered, and she swallowed hard, unsure of what her answer should be.

The music stopped, making her reply unnecessary, as they made their way back to the table in the alcove.

Ramon ordered liqueurs and as they waited, she noticed his eyes skim round the room. He seemed strangely on edge, expectant, his expression tense.

'Would you rather we left now?' she asked, noticing his tension increase with every passing second.

'No, we must celebrate the free evening,' he declared. 'You are not too tired?'

'Oh no, I'm fine, it's just that you seem a little on edge. I wondered if you were wanting to leave.'

'To the contrary, I am delighted your previous appointment was cancelled, leaving you free for the evening.'

She started inwardly. How did Ramon know of her previous engagement, and did he realise it was to have been with Mark? Ramon's eyes were upon her, and he obviously expected her to enlighten him further. She took a shaky breath. 'I was going to the theatre but there were no tickets available.'

'And your escort had no alternative to offer you?' he asked.

'He had a business appointment,' she explained.

'I see.' Ramon remained outwardly calm, yet she sensed he held his innermost feelings tightly reined.

She glanced up suddenly as the head waiter came towards their table and stopped to speak to Ramon in a discreet whisper.

'He asks if we desire anything more,' Ramon explained, in response to her enquiring glance, before reaching for her hand. 'Shall we dance again?'

Was Ramon really enjoying the evening or merely being polite in ensuring she didn't miss out on any of the activities, she wondered, as he led her round the outside of the now crowded floor.

Suddenly she felt his grip tighten on her hand as he spoke. 'Whatever happens, Vicky, I hope you will not think too harshly of me in the future. Look straight ahead,' he directed, turning her to face the tables surrounding the floor.

She frowned slightly at his odd request, and viewed the area he indicated, then she got the full shocking impact. There was one face she recognised, a familiar face, smiling confidently.

'Mark!' she gasped, but the music drowned her exclamation, and he remained unaware of her standing there as he lifted a glass to his lips, his attention focussed on the woman who clung possessively to his arm.

Vicky watched as Mark's lips came to rest on his companion's cheek. She wanted to turn and run, but Ramon felt her tense in his arms, and his grip tightened, imprisoning her, forcing her to witness a spectacle which wounded her deeply.

She saw the woman at Mark's side laugh, her red lips parting provocatively. She was quite beautiful and perfectly groomed, but even the well placed make-up and the expensive clothes couldn't hide the fact she must be Mark's senior by at least twenty years, and he was gazing at her adoringly.

Vicky closed her eyes to blot out the sight of their smiling faces. Ramon had planned it this way, calmly leading her into a cruel trap, knowing it would be painful. Her heart pounded wildly as the colour drained from her face, and she fought for control over her shaking limbs as she faced him. 'Please, let me leave,' she said unsteadily, struggling to free herself from his iron grip.

Retaining his hold on her, Ramon led her swiftly to their table where he snatched up her bag and wrap, and, with a nod of acknowledgement towards the manager, firmly escorted her outside to his waiting car.

'I am very sorry, Vicky,' he murmured softly, 'but you had to know. I could not bear to stand by and see you enamoured of a man who is so obviously wrong for you.'

'How could you humiliate me like this?' she demanded.

'Come,' he replied briskly, 'get into the car. I expected a reaction like this. I knew you would be annoyed with me. I really do regret you had such an ordeal to suffer and I admired your composure at the time, but by now, you must realise he is nothing more than a gigolo. He was using you, and I am positive I know the reason,' he added, cryptically.

A tense silence lay between them throughout the journey, but she sensed his gaze rested on her occasionally as they covered the quiet road and she fought to control the tears, hating him for the pain and humiliation he caused her. This was more than she could bear and the sooner the time came to leave his home the better. Hopefully, during the final week, she could avoid any contact with him whatsoever, and it would mean using her wits if she was to keep the outcome of this evening from his mother's notice.

* * *

Vicky was grateful for Ramon's absence from the villa over the following weekend, and to her surprise, Senora Varela asked little about the evening of the flamenco dancing.

As she supposed, there was no telephone call from Mark on Monday morning, and she restrained her desire to contact him and challenge him with how he had spent Friday evening. Without doubt, he would be armed with a number of excuses which would only serve to provoke her into retaliating with what she knew to be the truth. Her pride had suffered a shattering blow, but once the humiliation had lessened, she experienced no great longing to either hear or see him again.

Guiltily, she recalled how she had challenged Ramon accusingly and disregarded his sympathy. He'd asked her not to think too harshly of him in the future, whatever happened.

Curiously, she found it extremely pleasant to recall the happier times spent in Ramon's company, but the chances of repeating such ecstatic moments were extremely remote, and she had only herself to blame.

Suddenly, she wanted to keep the bracelet he had given her, desperately needing to retain a memento of the most precious moments of her life. She turned from the balcony as a tap sounded on the door of her room.

'Yes, come in,' she invited, and hastily brushed the tears from her cheeks as Tina entered.

'The senora wishes me to inform you lunch will be half an hour later as the doctor will not be dining in today,' Tina imparted, in cool tones.

'Thank you. Do come in,' Vicky added.

Tina hesitated in the doorway. 'I am rather busy.'

'Surely you can spare a few minutes? After all, I won't have the opportunity to spend much more time with you, there are only a few days left now.'

Tina returned sharply, 'You are happy to go, no?'

'Tina!' Vicky exclaimed, and to her dismay, saw tears fill the other woman's eyes. 'Whatever's the matter?'

'I will be happy when you go,' Tina blurted out.

Perturbed by the resentment in Tina's voice, Vicky appealed to her. 'Tina, we've always been friends. Tell me, what's wrong?'

'You have made him so unhappy, it is better you go!' Tina cried, her voice shrill. 'You bring only trouble to this house.'

'Please, Tina,' Vicky entreated. 'Who have I made unhappy? Do you mean Doctor Varela? Please, come and sit down and tell me.'

'Thank you, no. You know the doctor has been almost ill with worry, but you turn away from him. You do not care.'

'Worried. About me?' Vicky gasped.

'Yes, of course, about you,' the woman cried passionately. 'You are so blind! Why do you think he stays away from the villa now?'

'Just a minute. Why are you so upset about this? Has someone been talking to you about me? Tell me, please,' Vicky implored. 'Why is the doctor so worried?'

'I am not listening, you understand? But I hear them talking, I cannot help it. They talk about you and that man, Gildner, so I think you are like the other companion. You would have allowed him into the villa if the doctor had not prevented it.'

Vicky stared, open-mouthed in amazement, and deeply concerned over Tina's fierce accusations. What was the mystery surrounding her predecessor to cause this hurtful verbal assault from Tina?

'You'd better explain, Tina, obviously there's more to all this than I'd realised. I can't bear to think I'm the cause of any trouble here. Please, tell me what the other companion did?'

'You really do not know? Then perhaps it is better you understand. It was because of Lisa the last companion. He liked her,' Tina continued sadly, 'until he found out.'

'Found out what?'

'About Lisa and the robbery here.'

'Robbery,' Vicky cried. 'You mean she stole from here?'

'Yes, Lisa took Senora Varela's jewels, her beautiful sapphire necklace and the valuable paintings from the walls of the villa. Doctor Varela would not believe his mother in the beginning, until the day he saw Lisa, in a bar. She was with two men, giving them the jewel box, the one with the necklace.'

'Oh, how terrible for him.'

'Yes, he had been called there, the proprietor's child was ill. It was lucky he should see.'

'So he challenged them?'

'No, he had to attend to the emergency of

the child's illness first, and they had left. But another day he stayed here while his mother took her siesta, and Lisa did not know, she thought he was at the surgery. He watched her signal from the balcony to a waiting taxi, then the cook opened the door to the men who came for the paintings.'

Vicky realised the sapphire necklace was probably the one she herself had worn the evening Ramon had taken her to Tarragona. She recalled how he had looked at it with unconcealed surprise, and no wonder. The necklace the police had delivered to his consulting rooms beforehand; the necklace Senora Varela didn't expect to see again.

A sudden chill ran along her spine. Mark had shown an exceptional interest in the villa's contents, a great desire to view its valuable paintings and antiques. Mark had very nearly fooled her!

'Ah Vicky, it was terrible,' Tina said passionately. 'Of course he sent her away immediately, the cook and her husband also, but they did terrible things to him that day. You have seen the scar, no? It was so bad, they shaved off his beard.'

Vicky gasped. 'The scar, yes, I've noticed. They did that?'

'Yes, he challenged the men here, at the villa, but they fought him with a knife. He was unconscious for a long time, and so ill.' Tina wrung her hands, agitated by the memory of the event. 'And Lisa swore he had given her the jewels. She told the police he was her betrothed.'

'Surely the police realised it was not the truth?' Vicky said.

'It could not be proved, and Lisa said he must drop the charges otherwise his mother would be in danger.'

'Lisa threatened him?'

'Yes, he was so shocked by her behaviour, and fearing for his mother's life, he ordered the villa to be closed, and the senora must go to a hotel where she would be safe while the police made their arrests. It was then that he heard of the man, Gildner, one of a gang who make money by paying servants to let them into the houses of rich people. They are terrible people, Vicky, they do not work. They live on the riches of others.'

'It must have been really dreadful for him, but I'm glad you have finally told me everything,' Vicky told the other woman.

It became very clear to her why Ramon hadn't revealed his identity in the beginning. He had wanted to observe the new companion closely, but for a reason she couldn't appreciate at the time. She now realised how deeply he must have suffered.

Vicky now made an attempt at cheerfulness. 'Tina, what about the flowers, the carnations. You never did tell me what was so special about them.'

'Ah, we call them Clavel, and in the happy days here, before Doctor Varela's trouble, he would bring them to the house, some for every room. He called them the flower of peace and happiness, and when I saw some here in your room, I hoped it was true.'

'Oh, I see,' Vicky whispered, her thoughts quickly returning to the first bouquet he had presented to her, and the flowers he had chosen on behalf of his patient. She recalled his admission as they returned from visiting the hospital that he did not wish to be hurt again. Tortured by the deception of her predecessor, he tested her whilst acting under an assumed name, fearful of a recurrence.

The following morning, Ramon had slipped away, robbing her of the chance to speak with him over breakfast. Later, Vicky drove into Sitges and parked by the bank in the square hopeful of finding him there. His car was nowhere to be seen.

Driving away from the town, she steered towards the narrow winding road of the hill. At the second bend she noticed a small gathering of people walking ahead, and a policeman on a motorcycle overtook her as she drew closer.

She slowed down, and only when passing the group to round the next bend did she have a clearer view up the hill. There ahead, at the roadside, becoming clearly visible as she drew closer, were the crashed vehicles—a large lorry, its load of stone spilling over, deeply embedded into a long and familiar black car.

Horror struck, chilling her to the bone—she knew it to be Ramon's car! Braking sharply at the scene, as the colour drained from her face, she ran over to the mangled wreckage, finding no sign of the driver of either vehicle. Her legs barely supported her as she looked around. What had happened? Where was Ramon?

She cried, 'Where is the driver?' as the policeman pulled his machine on to its stand.

She heard him speak rapidly to another man who had reached the scene, a man who spoke loudly and excitedly. At the uniformed man's command he paused and extended his arm in the direction of the villa, shaking his head despairingly.

Suddenly, in that one fleeting moment she knew, undoubtedly, she cared about Ramon more than anything; loved him with every beat of her heart. But did the man's expression of despair mean it was too late?

Dashing back to her car she quickly accelerated up the hill, swerving recklessly, tyres screeching on the bend.

The iron gates of Villa Barca loomed before her, partly opened, and she tore towards them, swerving narrowly between, the gravel cracking beneath the tyres as she swung the little car round the drive. Braking violently, she flung the door wide and alighted shakily. Reaching the terrace, she almost fell into the arms of the man standing in her path.

He held her, and his eyes widened in surprise. 'Vicky!'

'Ramon!' Sobs of relief racked her whole being.

'Vicky, whatever is the matter?' he asked sharply, holding her trembling body in his strong grip.

'Your car—I thought—' she faltered, shaking her head—as the words caught in her throat. 'I thought you were hurt.' Speechless, as the relief of knowing he was safe flooded through her body, she clung to him for support, and Ramon held her tightly to him, murmuring softly until her trembling subsided.

Gently he lifted her chin, and looking searchingly into her glistening blue eyes, asked, 'You were worried because I may have been injured, Vicky? You really cared?'

She nodded, biting her lower lip to control its quivering, and a look of relief flooded his dark eyes. His arms enfolded her, holding her shaking body close to his own.

'My little English nurse,' he murmured huskily, 'I am very happy to know you care so much.'

'But your car, Ramon,' she quavered. 'What happened?'

'It had broken down, so I left it beside the road and walked up to the villa to telephone the garage. During that time the lorry crashed into it. I had just returned here for the second time, after inspecting the damage, when I heard your car coming so speedily through the gates.'

'Oh.' She sighed with relief. 'I thought you were inside the car when it crashed. Oh, Ramon, what a shock I got! It was dreadful to see your car so badly wrecked; it's terribly smashed and broken.'

'Not as badly broken as my heart was, Vicky,' he said quietly, holding her at arm's length so that she couldn't avoid seeing the anguish in his dark eyes.

She lowered her glance, catching a glimpse of the jagged scar beneath his chin. 'Yes, I know. Tina told me,' she admitted softly.

'Tina?'

Vicky nodded. 'Yes, and I'm so sorry. You should have told me about Lisa and all the trouble you had. I would have understood, Ramon, and you could have relied on my discretion. I hope you didn't mind her telling me. I almost dragged the truth out of her, and now I realise you must have—'

'No, Vicky.' He shook her, gently. 'Not for Lisa, or the trouble here at the villa. My heart was broken because of you, and—'

'And Mark Gildner?'

'Yes, I must admit I was jealous, but though I didn't want to hurt you, I had to make you see him for what he was, and there was no other way. I couldn't bear to think of you with that unscrupulous devil!'

'And you were right about him. Oh, Ramon,

I have been so foolish.'

'No, darling, don't blame yourself, he was a confidence trickster, you were not to know. And he didn't recognise me without my beard, on the night of the concert,' Ramon added.

'Can you ever forgive my stupidity? I didn't realise why you appeared so unreasonable.'

Pulling her close once more, he said tenderly, 'I love you, and I believe you once loved me but I spoiled it, I hurt you. Can you ever love me again? Even though I had to deceive you, you remained loyal.'

'Yes, Ramon,' she answered, tears of happiness sparkling in her eyes, 'now I know I have loved you all the time.'

'I should have told you who I was in the beginning,' he admitted huskily, a slight smile curving his lips as he gazed down at her, 'but, my middle name is Ramon.'

The weight had been lifted from her heart and she could only smile up at him happily, knowing his name mattered little. It was the man she loved—Paul Ramon Varela.

His lips brushed hers before he asked, 'You will marry me, my little Clavel? We are already promised to each other by the bracelet. You have not returned it.'

'By the bracelet?' she queried, remembering Tina had said something about its meaning. 'I haven't thanked you properly I know, and it's so beautiful, but has it some really special meaning?'

'Yes. Years ago, I believe it was the custom in this country for a gentleman to give a bracelet to the young lady he wished to marry. Maybe it will suffice until I bring a ring for your finger as is the present day arrangement, that is,' he raised a dark brow questioningly, 'if you have decided to stay?'

Yes, Ramon,' she whispered, 'deep in my heart, I never wanted to leave.'